THE AEGIS KEY
Written by T.O.Tryon

ISBN-979-8-0033119-1-3

Written by T.O.TRYON
Cover and Illustration by T.O.TRYON

IN MEMORY OF

LYNNE TRYON

In the late 1800s, Nikola Tesla claimed to hear something no one else could—a pulse in the void, faint and rhythmic, like a beacon meant for no human ear. He believed it was a message from the stars, a signal meant to be answered. Others dismissed it as folly, the ramblings of a dreamer obsessed with lightning.

But Tesla wasn't the last to hear it.

Decades later, military satellites caught the same whisper. High above the Earth, in a patch of sky thought to be empty, something vast and cold drifted in silence. It has been called many names across the years—messenger, ghost, harbinger. None of them quite fit.

The first recovery attempts were hurried and secret. Dark-winged capsules carrying brave men were launched toward the silent intruder.   None returned alive.

Their bodies came back scorched, or worse—frozen husks drifting through orbit, their faces locked in screams that would never fade.

Every expedition since has ended the same way: failure, death, silence. And yet, it still waits. Patient. Watching.

Some say it has been there for thousands of years. Others claim it arrived only recently. Whatever the truth, one fact remains: humanity is not alone in the dark. And the dark is waiting.

Chapter 1
The Boy and His Dirtbike

September, 10, 1995

The dirtbike's engine coughed, then roared to life as Jack Tengu twisted the throttle as his studded tires ripped across the cracked gravel road. The September air was sharp against his cheeks, the faint smell of cut hay drifting from the fields.

Behind him, the sun hung low, painting the horizon with bruised streaks of purple and gold.

Jack leaned into the curve, the back tire skidding just enough to make the bike buck like a wild thing. He grinned at the sound, a reckless flash of joy in a life that rarely left room for it. The faster he went, the less he thought of his foster parents and the stink of cheap whiskey waiting for him back home, or the bruises he covered up at school, or the hollow space where sober parents were supposed to be.

At the front of the high school, he throttled down, letting the engine growl into silence. Kids milling near the steps looked up, some with smirks, others with rolled eyes.

Jack swung a leg off the bike, leather jacket creasing as he tugged the helmet free. His black hair stuck in wild tufts, and he shook it out with practiced carelessness.

"Subtle as always," Gemma called, already waiting by the steps. Her voice carried that teasing warmth Jack craved, and when she smiled, it was like she'd stolen the sun from the sky and kept it for herself.

Jack's grin softened. "What can I say? We're seniors, I gotta show the young punks how to look good."

She tucked a strand of auburn hair behind her ear, narrowing her eyes playfully. "You're a young punk, Jack."

"Ah ah, you can't say that anymore... we're 18 now." Jack shot back. He let her slide into step beside him, her hand caressing his.

Chris Weaver arrived in his usual tangle of limbs, glasses askew, clutching a notebook crammed with diagrams and loose sheets.

He was already talking before he reached them.

"Did you guys hear about the object they saw over Nevada last week? Not military. Not weather balloons. Some astronomer swears it wasn't a comet either—"

"Morning to you too, Chris," Jack interrupted.

Chris blinked, then smiled sheepishly. "Right. Morning. But I'm serious. There are patterns in the sky lately. Something's moving up there."

Jack arched a brow. "You've been up all night again, haven't you?"

Chris didn't answer, which was answer enough. Gemma sighed but squeezed his shoulder. "One day, Chris, your brain is going to combust from the sheer amount of useless trivia you cram into it."

"Not useless," he muttered, clutching his notebook tighter. "Not if it's true."

The bell rang, pulling them toward the building.

Classes blurred by the way they always did, a haze of teachers' voices, slamming lockers, the stale tang of cafeteria pizza. Jack walks into a bathroom as the local burnouts pin Chris against the wall.

Jack immediately punches one of them in the ribs and they back off after realizing it was Jack, and leave quickly.

"You really gotta start sticking up for yourself, Man." Jack says picking up Chris's books. The bell rings.

After school, Jack walked Gemma out to the bike. The autumn wind had picked up, carrying the distant barking of dogs and the faint roar of farm trucks on back roads.

Gemma slid on behind him, arms snug around his waist, and Jack revved the engine, as they drove off together.

In the heart of a nearby clearing, ripples in the air shivered, bending inward as if the world itself were drawing breath.

With a low hum, a swirling vortex of light and shadow yawned open between the trees, scattering leaves in a frantic spiral.

From its depths, a small armored humanoid emerged soundlessly, her armor catching faint glimmers of sparks of as the portal pulsed behind her.

A guttural snarl shakes the leaves. Out of the swirling light, rises a hulking form of a huge gnashing beast. It pulls itself from the violet rift, claws gouging the soil.

The monster snarled viciously, eyes burning with insane rage as the tall ears pricked up on the small armored being, and she turned her helm just slightly. No words passed—only a gesture, sharp and precise.

At once the beast's growl deepened, and

with a furious bellow it leapt into the forest, shaking the ground with its thunderous charge as the clearing fell silent once more.

For a few miles, the world shrank to the engine's hum and the warmth of her pressed against his back.

They parked in front of her house, a neat place with flowerbeds and curtains that matched. Jack lingered a moment longer than he needed to, tugging at his gloves, staring at the porch light flicking on.

"You'll be okay tonight?" she asked quietly. Jack shrugged, forcing a smirk. "Always am."

"Jack…" Her hand caught his. Her eyes searched his face, trying to read what he wouldn't say out loud.

He kissed her quickly, before words could spoil it. When he pulled away, she smiled faintly, though her eyes still carried that worry she never quite hid.

"See you tomorrow," he said, kicking the bike to life.

"Promise?" She stood on the porch as he pulled away, her silhouette fading in the rear view until there was nothing but road and fields again.

Night deepened fast in the country. The

dirt road stretched long and lonely beneath the thin wash of moonlight. Jack gunned the engine, headlights bouncing across uneven ruts, the cool air biting sharper now. Gravel and dust spitting from the back tire on the gravel road.

Jack rode unknowing... He didn't see the snarling shadow that detached itself from the treeline. Didn't notice the way it slithered across the ditch and matched his speed, silent and powerful.

By the time he reached the battered barn behind his foster house, his mind was already turning toward the bike's engine rattle that he wanted to fix. He killed the engine, rolled the bike inside, and leaned it against the workbench.

The barn smelled of hay, oil and rust, the old rafters groaning with every gust of wind. He knelt, hands already busy with tools, humming tunelessly under his breath.

Outside, in the long grass, something shifted.

It watched through the crack in the boards, eyes glinting faintly in the dark. The boy didn't look up. The wrench clinked against metal. An owl cawed in the distance and went silent. The thing waited. Silent.

Chapter 2
The Hunter in the Barn

The wrench slipped, scraping Jack's knuckles. He hissed, stuck his hand in his mouth, and muttered a curse under his breath. A smear of grease darkened his skin, joining the constellation of half-healed scrapes that are already on display.

He leaned back on his heels, examining the carburetor with the stubborn patience of someone who refused to let machines win.

The mud covered dirt bike had become his refuge; it didn't judge, didn't scream, didn't stumble through the door, it put him down or hit him with a bottle in it's hand.

It only broke down, and when it did, Jack could fix it.

The barn creaked with the shifting night. The rafters whispered, the loose boards tapped against one another in the wind.

He tuned it out, the way he always did. But this time, the sounds didn't stop. Something brushed against the outer wall. A dragging, deliberate scrape.

Jack froze, wrench clutched tight in his fist. His pulse hammered. Probably a raccoon. Or a stray dog nosing around.

Then came the thud. Heavy. Slow. Too heavy for a raccoon.

The hair on his neck prickled.

Jack pushed to his feet, eyes scanning the shadows. The weak bulb overhead flickered once, twice, then steadied with a faint buzz. He told himself not to be stupid, but his body didn't listen; his muscles locked, breath shallow.

From the far corner, darkness shifted. The shape uncoiled, slithering forward with a wet scrape across the concrete floor. A shimmer of pale, glistening skin caught the light before it darted back into shadow.

Jack's chest seized.

The thing stepped into the light.

It's body was wrong—limbs too long, joints bending backward, head low and narrow with teeth like broken glass jutting from black gums.

The eyes burned faintly red, unblinking. Strings of saliva dripped from its jaws, hissing when they hit the floor.

For a heartbeat, neither moved.

Then it lunged.

Jack snatched the first thing his hand found: the shovel propped against the workbench. The creature hit him hard, knocking him into the wooden beam.

Pain exploded across his shoulder. He swung the shovel with all the strength his wiry frame could muster.

The blade connected with the creature's face with a crunch. It screeched, high and shrill, the sound splitting Jack's skull. The force staggered it but didn't stop it.

It whipped a clawed hand across Jack's stomach. Hot agony tore him open. He gasped, stumbling back, hands clutching his abdomen as blood spilled between his fingers.

His knees buckled.

The world blurred at the edges. The creature loomed, snarling, saliva dripping onto the floorboards beside him.

Jack tried to lift the shovel again, but his arms were lead. His vision swam.

The monster lunged—

—and the window behind Jack exploded inward.

A ball of searing light shot into the barn, humming like a thousand wasps. It hovered above him, a sphere no larger than a basketball, smooth and black with shifting veins of blue light crawling across its surface.

The creature shrieked and lunged toward it. The orb flared. A beam of white light blasted from its core, striking the monster mid-leap.

The thing dissolved in an instant—skin, bone, warbling shriek—all crumbling to ash that scattered on the barn floor.

Jack stared, breath ragged, blood hot against his hands.

The orb hovered closer, bathing him in its glow.

He tried to crawl backward, but his limbs failed. His eyelids sagged, too heavy to keep open.

The last thing he saw before darkness swallowed him was his spurting, blood-soaked shirt, and his torn flesh held desperately together by his shaking hand. The orb pulsed once, twice—then everything went black.

Chapter 3
The Aegis Core

Jack jerked awake, choking on a breath that burned like fire in his chest.

He wasn't in the barn. He wasn't anywhere he knew.

He sat up too fast, nearly sliding off the slab beneath him. It wasn't a bed—it was a black, floating platform, smooth as glass, humming faintly beneath his hands.

His eyes darted around. The room curved in ways his brain didn't like—walls that bent seamlessly into ceiling and floor, no seams, no corners. The surfaces were slick and black, like polished stone, but pulsed faintly with threads of blue light that crawled beneath the skin of the ship, as if the whole place were alive.

"A nightmare?—" His voice cracked. He tried again. "Where the hell am I?"

A sound answered him.

Wet. Squirming. And getting closer.

Jack froze, head snapping toward the noise. A shadow darted across his chest.

Something cold and damp pressed against his cheek. He yelped and swatted instinctively. A slimy, translucent slug—its body glowing faintly blue—slid across his face. Its little feelers twitched as if in curiosity.

Jack scrambled up, gagging. "What the --?!"

The thing clung to his jaw, leaving a trail of goo. He flung it as hard as he could. It slapped wetly against the wall, billowing an obscene noise of trapped gasses within it.

The sound echoed absurdly in the alien chamber.

Jack blinked, horrified and confused in equal measure. The slug wriggled, then oozed off the wall as if nothing had happened.

"Abducted by aliens and assaulted by a farting booger... a dream?... too much carb cleaner?" Jack chuckles nervously and wipes his face with his sleeve. "WHAT THE HELL IS GOING ON!?"

Movement stirred at the far end of the chamber.

Something poured out of the wall. At first it looked like a swarm of black cables spilling like liquid, writhing and twisting over one another.

They coiled together, rising and weaving into a vaguely human shape. Limbs. Shoulders. A head with no face.

Jack staggered backward until his spine

pressed against the wall. His pulse thundered. "Oh shit! Stay the hell away from me."

The writhing mass then spoke to Jack in a strange language that sounded like static and serrated thunder.

The dark figure advanced. Its cables lashed out, faster than his eyes could follow. They wrapped around his wrists, his chest, pinning him in place. He thrashed, kicked, swore.

One of the tendrils darted for his neck. He shouted, jerking his head aside—but the needle-thin tip plunged into the skin beneath his ear. A burning sting shot through him.

Jack gasped. His knees buckled. The fight drained from his muscles.

His ears rang—then the ringing turned into something else.

A voice.

Smooth, female, calm. "You are safe. Do not be afraid."

Jack's head snapped up. The faceless mass still writhed in front of him, but the voice filled his mind as if it had always been there.

"What—what the hell are you?"

The cables loosened, lowering him gently

back onto the slab.

"I am Broken1," the voice said.
"Emergency construct of the Aegis Core. I was created to protect you."

Jack's breath came ragged, his eyes flicking down to his shirt. He froze.

The blood was gone. The gash across his stomach—where claws had raked him open—was nothing but smooth, pale skin beneath the tear in his shirt.

"No…!" His voice cracked. "That's not possible. I was—!" He pressed his hands against the place where the wound had been, desperate to feel the pain that wasn't there.

The voice softened. "You were dying. I repaired you."

He staggered to his feet. "Repaired me? What the hell are you talking about? Where am I?"

The cables shifted, pointing toward a doorway that peeled open in the black wall. Beyond it stretched a hallway glowing with faint blue veins, leading into deeper shadows.

"You are aboard the Aegis Core" Broken1 said. "An orbiting vessel above your world. We do not have much time, Jack Tengu."

The sound of his own name in that alien

voice made the hair rise on his arms. He looked from the open hallway to the faceless construct.

"You… know me."

"I know everything about you," Broken1 replied. "You were made for this."

Jack backed toward the doorway, every instinct screaming to run, even though there was nowhere to run to.

At the end of the hall, the black wall split open again, revealing a vast chamber beyond.

Jack stepped through—and froze.

The space was colossal, a cathedral of alien technology. Smooth black surfaces curved into sweeping arches, blue light pulsing like veins. In the center, banks of shifting symbols rippled across panels Jack couldn't begin to understand. And beyond it all—

—a window.

A raw cut of space itself, staring down at Earth. The blue curve of the planet hung in the darkness, clouds trailing across its face like smoke.

Jack staggered forward, drawn to it. His stomach flipped as vertigo threatened to drag him forward into the abyss.

"Is this... for real?" Jack stammers.

Behind him, Broken1's voice whispered, softer now, almost tender:
"You are home, Jack. And you are not who you think you are."

Chapter 4
Broken1's Truth

Jack's hands gripped the railing that wasn't a railing at all—it simply grew out of the floor, curving upward as though the ship had decided he needed something to hold onto.

The silent Earth floated beyond the opening, blue and fragile, a marble slowly spinning in the black ocean. He stared so long his eyes burned.

"This isn't real," he muttered. "This can't be real."

The faceless construct slithered into the chamber behind him, its black cables weaving with quiet grace. Its presence filled the space like smoke.

"It is real," the voice said. Smooth. Patient. Like a nurturing female. "You are in orbit, Jack. You are aboard the Aegis Core."

Jack spun, pointing a finger at it like a weapon. "Stop saying my name. Stop acting like you know me."

"I do know you. I created you."The words struck harder than claws. Jack's stomach lurched.

"Bullshit."

The construct tilted its head without a

face. "Four million years ago, the Aegis was left in orbit as debris. Its parent vessel, The Aegis, departed, and never returned. The Core remained behind, failing, fragmenting, but not dying.

It waited. It needed a pilot. Without one, it could not search for its parent. So it made me. Broken1. My function was to create that pilot."

Jack's chest heaved. "And you're saying that's me? That you—what?—built me?"

"Yes."

The cables rippled, folding in and out of themselves like a sea anemone breathing. "From the last viable stock of organic nanites, I crafted a new design. Human, but more. DNA altered. Enhanced.

You were placed on the surface, hidden among them, to grow, to learn, to survive. You are the Aegis Core Pilot, Jack Tengu."

Jack laughed, sharp and cracked. "Yeah, right.

That's a hell of a story, pipe cleaner. Too bad I'm just some foster kid from nowhere who can't even keep a C average. You've got the wrong guy."

"You are precisely the right one."

Jack slammed a fist against the railing and hyperventilates. "No! I don't want this. I don't want any of this!"

The construct's cables twitched, agitated. The voice stayed calm. "You were never given the choice. You are necessary. Without you, the Aegis Core will fade. And the fate of the parent craft will remain unknown forever."

Jack's heart pounded. "Why me? Out of everyone on Earth—hell, out of the whole damn galaxy—why me?"

"You survived," Broken1 said simply. "Every trial, every hardship. You endured pain, abandonment, violence. Your spirit was forged in fire. You are clever, resourceful, stubborn. Human traits, refined through alien design. You are what the Aegis needs. Out of all of my attempts, you have survived the longest. I hid you well, this time"

Jack shook his head, retreating a step. "No. I'm just a screw-up. I get into fights, I barely scrape through school, and—" His throat closed. "—and the only good thing I've got is Gemma. And Chris. I'm not leaving them behind because some… machine says I was made to fly a UFO!"

For the first time, silence filled the chamber.

Then Broken1's voice shifted, lower,

almost mournful.

"The Core is dying, Jack. I am dying. We have little time before I fail completely. If you do not accept your purpose, both of us, and the Aegis Core will perish.

...The hunters will come. They now know you exist. I am sorry, if you do not fulfill your destiny. You will not survive long."

Jack swallowed hard. The memory of the creature in the barn—the claws, the blood, the way it dissolved in the orb's beam—flashed in his mind.

His voice was hoarse when he spoke. "That thing… in the barn. It wasn't the first, was it?"

"No. It will not be the last. More will follow. They will not stop until you are dead, and the Key is lost."

Jack's hands tightened on the railing. His reflection in the black surface of the wall looked like a stranger—pale, wide-eyed, trembling.

"I didn't ask for this," he whispered.

"No one asks for destiny," Broken1 said gently. "But some are fortunate enough to be made for it."

Jack closed his eyes, jaw clenched. Panic rising. He then turned sharply toward the open hall, toward anywhere that wasn't

that uncanny voice, this ship, this
nightmare.

"I don't care. I'm not your pilot. I'm not
your savior. I'm not anything but me!"
He started walking.

Broken1's cables writhed, reaching after
him but stopping short. The voice followed,
softer now, echoing through the alien
chamber:

"You cannot run forever, Jack Tengu. You
are the only one who can find the Key."
Jack didn't look back.

Chapter 5
Shadows in the Sky

Gemma Collins tapped her fingernails against the cafeteria table, staring at the untouched apple on her tray. Chris Weaver sat across from her, bent over a notebook filled with equations that had no place in a high school lunchroom.

"He's not answering," Gemma said frantically, voice tight. "I've called his house three times. His foster dad mumbled that he never came inside last night."

Chris didn't look up. "Maybe his dirt bike broke down. Maybe he's camping out somewhere."

"You don't believe that."

Chris's pencil froze mid-line. Slowly, he pushed the notebook away and met her eyes. His were tired, shadowed, but steady. "No. I don't."

Gemma pulled her jacket tighter around herself though the room was warm.

A knot of unease coiled in her stomach, one that had been growing since Jack dropped her off the night before.

She'd seen something in his eyes then—something unspoken, like he'd been carrying a secret too heavy to share.

She bit her lip. "What if he's in real trouble, Chris?"

Chris didn't answer, because he didn't have to. They both knew trouble followed Jack Tengu like a shadow. But this time felt different.

Two hundred miles away, in a secure facility buried beneath Cheyenne Mountain, a bank of monitors bathed a darkened control room in pale green light. Satellite images flickered across the screens: infrared sweeps, radar feeds, and one particularly grainy still frame of a streak of fire cutting through the night sky over Kansas.

General Mason stood with his arms folded behind his back, the stiff lines of his uniform sharp as blades. His eyes, cold and gray, lingered on the holographic images.

"Trajectory?" he asked.

"Unknown, sir," replied Agent Weiss, standing at his shoulder. The younger man's face was unreadable, every word clipped. "But we have confirmation of an object entering low orbit.

It matches nothing in the catalog. Not Russian. Not Chinese. Definitely not ours... an Orb."

Mason's lips tightened into something between a smile and a snarl. "And the anomalous energy spike?"

Weiss handed him a file. Inside were grainy photos: strange readings from ground sensors, electrical disturbances in a rural county, a barn camera catching a blurry shape before going black.

"Localized to a fifteen-mile radius," Weiss said. "We've dispatched retrieval teams, but… the trail's gone cold."

Mason closed the file with deliberate care. His voice was low, almost reverent. "It's happening again."

Weiss inclined his head. "You think it's connected to the Key?"

"I don't think," Mason said. "I know." He turned toward the wall-sized map glowing with surveillance markers. His reflection loomed on the screen: a soldier who looked more like a predator. "Dark Wing recovery team is authorized." he ordered.

"Lock down the area, silence the locals, and find me whatever fell from the sky. If the Aegis Core is stirring after all these years…"

His grin was sharp and humorless.

"…then the game has finally begun again."

Back in Kansas, Gemma stared out the

classroom window as the day dragged on. A contrail of a jet split the sky overhead. She shivered without knowing why. Something told her Jack wasn't just in trouble.

Chapter 6
Ashes in the Barn

Agent Weiss crouched in the pasture, the beam of his flashlight sweeping over the carcass of a cow. Its body was stiff, eyes wide, a deep wound carved through its hide as if by blades. Steam still curled faintly from the flesh. A white enviro-suited scientist takes a tissue sample.

Weiss touched the blackened edge of the wound with a gloved finger. The residue shimmered faintly under the light, unnatural.

"Not coyotes," he muttered. "Not anything from this planet."

He rose, eyes narrowing toward the silhouette of a leaning barn at the edge of the field. His men spread out behind him, sweeping the dark with disciplined precision.

The barn door groaned open at his touch. Inside, the air was thick with the stench of oil and scorched metal. His light passed over tools, stacks of hay, a dirt bike half-disassembled. Then he stopped.

At the center of the floor lay a mound of fine black ash, faintly iridescent under the light. Beside it leaned a shovel, its blade slick with something that wasn't rust. Thick streaks of blood so dark it looked black.

Weiss knelt, staring at the ash as though it might breathe. He pinched a bit between his fingers, rubbed it. The grains shimmered faintly, then dissolved like smoke.

"Confirmed," he whispered. His mouth tightened into something almost like satisfaction.

Gemma's heart pounded as she and Chris walked the dirt road toward Jack's house. The place loomed ahead, weathered and lonely under the Oklahoma moon.

"Maybe this is a bad idea," Chris muttered, clutching his backpack straps like a shield.

"We're not leaving without checking," Gemma said firmly. Her voice trembled anyway.

They crept through the yard, past the silent farmhouse, toward the barn where Jack always parked his dirt bike. The door stood half open, light spilling from inside.

Gemma froze. "Someone's here."

Before Chris could reply, a voice drifted out —smooth, calm, but edged like a knife.

"Interesting timing."

A tall man stepped into view, suit immaculate despite the dust, eyes sharp as glass. The beam of his flashlight swung lazily over them, not blinding, just probing. "Evening," Agent Weiss said. "You two know the boy who lives here?"

Gemma's throat went dry. "Jack? Yeah, but—he's not home."

Weiss tilted his head, studying her face with unsettling patience. "No. He's not." He gestured behind him toward the pile of ash. "But something was."

Chris forced a nervous laugh. "Looks like… uh, looks like burned hay to me."

Weiss's smile was faint, humorless. He stepped closer, the light lingering on Chris's glasses, then on Gemma's clenched fists.

"You seem nervous," he said casually, as though commenting on the weather. "Did you see anything strange last night? Lights? Animals?"

Gemma met his gaze, forcing her voice steady. "No. Just Jack dropping me off across town. That's it."

Silence stretched. Weiss studied her a beat too long, like he could peel back the truth with his eyes alone. Then he gave a small nod, almost polite.

"Well. If you do… you'll tell me." It wasn't a question.

He stepped past them, boots crunching on the gravel, his men falling in behind him. The SUVs' engines rumbled to life outside.

Gemma exhaled only when the barn fell silent again. Her knees shook.

Chris whispered, "What the hell was that?"

Gemma stared at the black ash on the floor, her stomach twisting.

"Trouble," she said. "And I'm sure that Jack is in the middle of it."

Chapter 7
The Pact

Gemma's sneakers pounded against the gravel as she and Chris hurried down the road, the barn shrinking into the darkness behind them. Neither spoke until the glow of the SUVs faded into the horizon.

Finally, Chris wheezed, "We should not have been there."

"No kidding," Gemma shot back, her breath sharp. "But we had to be. Jack's in trouble, and now those guys know it too."

Chris tugged at his backpack strap like it was a nervous tic. "That man—Weiss—he knew we were lying. I could feel it. Like he was looking through me."

Gemma slowed, forcing him to meet her eyes. "We have to find Jack before that guy."

Chris blinked. "That's your plan?"

"It's the only plan until we find Jack."

The determination in her voice surprised even her. She wasn't used to being the one pulling Chris along—usually, it was Jack, dragging both of them into trouble. But now it was on her.

They lock the barn door. The space smelled of old paint and oil, stacked high with tools and half-finished projects. Chris flicked on a single desk lamp, casting the place in a circle of amber light.

Gemma dropped into a chair. "Okay. Talk. You're the brain here. What the hell happened back there?"

Chris rubbed his forehead. "The ash in the barn isn't natural. It dissolved—like it wasn't even solid. And the blood on the shovel…" He shivered. "Could be Jack's…"

Gemma's stomach clenched. "But if he was hurt that bad, where is he now?"

Chris leaned forward, eyes gleaming behind his glasses. "That's the thing. If Jack was bleeding out, he would've died right there. But he didn't.

Which means something—or someone—took him."

The room fell silent except for the hum of the lamp.

Gemma whispered, "So he's alive."

Chris nodded slowly. "I think so."

She gripped the table edge, steadying herself. "Then we're not giving up. Not ever."

Unseen from the street, a dark sedan idled two houses away. Inside, a man in a suit sat in the driver's seat, headset crackling faintly with static.

"Targets are in the barn," he murmured. "Orders?"

Through the earpiece came Agent Weiss's calm reply.

"Keep eyes on them. Don't interfere. If the boy makes contact, I want to know first."

The man lowered his headset, gaze fixed on the faint light spilling from the barn window. His expression was blank, professional.

And patient.

Chapter 8
Fall

The corridors of the Aegis Core swallowed sound. Black walls curved like muscle and bone, smooth yet alive with faint pulses of light. Jack's boots slapped against the seamless floor as he sprinted, heart hammering in his ears.

"Jack," the voice called from everywhere at once. Calm. Soothing. Relentless. "Please stop. You are not in danger."

"Leave me the hell alone!" he shouted, his voice echoing down the alien hall.

He turned a corner too fast, shoulder slamming into a wall that rippled faintly at the impact. He staggered, pushed off, kept running. The corridors shifted subtly as if the ship itself were rearranging to confuse him. Every intersection looked the same— black, smooth, endless.

Behind him came the low creeping and slithering of cables dragging across metal.

Broken1 followed without haste, every movement measured, inevitable.

"You must understand," she said, the voice vibrating in the walls and the floor. "You were created for this. Running does not change what you are."

Jack's breath came ragged. He didn't want explanations. He didn't want destiny. He wanted his dirt bike, his friends, his life.

He barreled through a final curve and stumbled into a chamber wider than the others. The far wall was dominated by a circular hatch.

Jack didn't think. He lunged for the hatch controls. Strange glyphs flared under his palm.

"No—" Broken1's voice sharpened, for the first time almost panicked.

The hatch irised open with a thunderclap. Vacuum roared. Jack was yanked off his feet, the air torn from his lungs as he was hurled into darkness.

Stars exploded around him, sharp and endless.

Below, the curve of Earth glowed blue and white, impossibly far, impossibly close.

He spun, limbs flailing uselessly, chest burning for air. A scream tore from his throat but vanished into the void.

Then—movement. Broken1 flung it's spiraling coils into the void after him.

From the gaping hatch behind him, the strange alien streaked across the emptiness, catching him just as he tumbled into the abyss.

Jack's vision blurred, fading. He felt the cold seep into his bones. Then something encased him, crawling over his arms, his chest, his face—black armor knitting together in an instant, like metal oil, seamless and alive. Blue lines flared across its surface, glowing like veins.

Air filled his lungs again, sharp and sweet. His body convulsed, gasping.

He looked down. The Earth was rushing up at him, clouds swirling like ghosts. He was falling.

But he wasn't dying.

The armor tightened around him, adjusting, guiding. Broken1's voice whispered in his ears, no longer calm, but urgent.

"Do not fight me, Jack. Trust me. You are not falling… you are descending."

Fire licked at the edges of his vision as they tore into the upper atmosphere, the sky igniting around him.

Jack screamed—not in terror, but in disbelief—as the world became fire and speed and the unstoppable pull of gravity.

Chapter 9
Impact

The night sky split open.

A streak of fire carved across the heavens, brighter than any falling star. Dogs barked across the county. Lights flicked on in farmhouses. And in a field just beyond the old barn, the ground shuddered. The raging ground spiraled in Jack's flashing visor as he screamed.

With a thunderous crack, Jack hit.

Dirt and flame exploded upward, showering the pasture in smoking soil. A crater gaped wide, molten at the edges. At its center lay a figure half-buried, black armor glowing with veins of electric blue. Steam hissed from every seam.

Jack groaned, rolling onto his side. His ears rang, his body ached, but he was alive. The armor felt like it was breathing with him, its pulse syncing with his racing heart.

He pushed himself up on trembling arms. Firelight licked off the blue-lit plating. For a moment he didn't even look human.

Gemma and Chris had been halfway down the long, dirt driveway when the sky tore open. Now they stood at the edge of the field, frozen.

"Chris," Gemma whispered, eyes wide, "I think that's… him."

Chris adjusted his glasses with a shaking hand. "Oh my God. That's Jack."

They took a step forward, but headlights swept across the dusk-fallen field. Black SUVs skidded to a stop surrounding Gemma and Chris, engines growling, doors slamming in perfect unison.

Dark figures spilled out, rifles low, movements sharp and professional.

At their head strode Agent Weiss, coat snapping in the hot wind of the crater. His eyes gleamed coldly as he took in the armored boy rising from the fire.

He lifted a radio to his lips. "Target confirmed. Alien tech confirmed. Orders?"

Static hissed. Then General Mason's voice crackled through, low and deliberate. "Stand down. Observe. Do not engage the subject.

"Weiss lowered the radio slowly. His gaze flicked to the tree line—where Gemma and Chris stood pale and exposed in the SUV lights.

He smiled faintly. "Understood."

Jack staggered to his feet, the black armor shifting with every motion, alive around him. His breath fogged inside the helmet, but he felt stronger than he ever had. He looked up—

—and saw Gemma and Chris.

Relief surged—only to turn to panic as Weiss snapped his fingers. Two agents swept forward, seizing the teens before they could run. Gemma screamed, kicking against their grip, while Chris shouted in protest.

Jack stumbled up the side of the crater. "No!"

Weiss opened the SUV door himself, ushering the struggling teens inside with unsettling calm.

He turned once, eyes meeting Jack's across the smoking field.

Then the doors slammed. Engines roared. The convoy peeled away into the night, taillights vanishing into darkness.

Jack reached the rim of the crater just in time to see the last SUV disappear down the road. His scream tore through the night, raw and furious.

"GEMMA! CHRIS!"

His voice echoed across the fields, swallowed by the smoke and silence. He dropped to his knees, fists clenched, armor humming with barely contained energy.

Jack Tengu realized the war for his life—and theirs—had just begun.

Chapter 10
The Weight of Fire

The crater smoldered around Jack, the earth cracked and blackened, the air thick with the acrid taste of smoke. Jack stood at its center, fists trembling, armor humming with restless energy. The field was silent now, save for the faint hiss of cooling soil. But the SUVs were gone.

Gemma's scream still echoed in his ears. Chris's terrified face burned into his mind. And he had done nothing.

His knees buckled. He fell, the armor clattering against the scorched ground. His breath came ragged, shallow. A sob broke from his chest, hot and ugly, before he could choke it back. He buried his face in his hands.

"They took them," he whispered. His voice cracked. "They took them and I couldn't stop it."

The armor receded, peeling back into black threads of liquid metal that slithered off his skin. They pooled on the ground, reshaping, reforming. Slowly, Broken1 rose again, a silhouette of cables and shifting limbs.

"Do not despair," the voice said gently.

Jack glared through the blur of tears. "Don't tell me not to despair! They're gone! My only family—the only people who matter—and you let it happen!"

Broken1 paused, as if the words cut deeper than expected. "I did not let it happen. I am limited.

The Core is weak. I saved you, Jack. I could not save them."

Jack shoved himself up, fists clenched. "Then what good are you? What's the point of all this if I can't protect them?"

The construct tilted her head. Its cables twisted inward, folding, compressing until its shape shrank. The mass reformed into a compact, sleek shape—black, angular, with faint blue lines like veins.

In seconds, it resembled a backpack, the straps rippling into place.

"Then use me," Broken1 said. Its voice was quieter now, almost weary. "Carry me. Together, we will find them. Together, we will fight."

Jack stared, chest heaving. Slowly, he bent down, picked up the strange weight, and slung it across his shoulders. It clung to him like it belonged there.

He turned toward the barn, its silhouette a familiar shape in the distance. He trudged across the field, boots sinking into the dirt, smoke curling behind him.

Inside, the dirtbike sat in pieces, tools scattered across the floor where he'd left them. He dropped onto the stool, staring at the mess.

"My bike's ruined," he muttered. "I can't even get into town, let alone after those bastards." His voice cracked again, bitter. "How the hell am I supposed to save anyone?"

For a moment, only silence. Then Broken1's voice, softer than he'd ever heard it:

"You are not alone anymore, Jack. You do not have to fix everything with your hands alone. You have me. And I will help you."

Jack looked down at his grease-stained fingers, then at the wreck of his bike. His jaw tightened.

"You better mean that," he said hoarsely.

"I do."

Jack exhaled slowly, staring at the broken machine. His heart ached with loss, with rage, but beneath it all was a spark—small, fragile, but alive.

Chapter 11
Passengers

The SUV's interior reeked of leather, gun oil, and cold air-conditioning. The hum of the engine vibrated through the floor, steady as a heartbeat. Outside the tinted windows, fields and farms slipped by in a blur of night.

Gemma sat pressed against the door, arms pinned by the steel grip of the agent beside her. Across the bench seat, Chris sat stiffly, hands clasped together in his lap as though in prayer.

His glasses had fogged from the sudden change of temperature, but his eyes burned with fury.

Neither spoke.

The driver didn't either, nor the two silent agents in the rear cargo seats. It was as if they were cargo—nothing more, nothing less.

Only one voice broke the silence.

"You both knew him."

Agent Weiss sat in the passenger seat, turned half-around to study them. His sharp profile glowed pale in the dashboard light, eyes cold and amused, like a man dissecting insects under glass.

Gemma's stomach tightened. "We don't know what you're talking about."

Weiss smiled faintly. "The boy in the crater. The one wrapped in alien technology." He leaned a little closer, voice smooth and conversational, as if they were at a dinner party. "You recognized him, I can only assume that was Jack."

Chris swallowed hard, then forced his voice steady. "We saw the same thing you did. A crash. Some… thing crawling out of it. That wasn't Jack."

Weiss studied him a long moment, his smile never faltering. "A clever lie. You're a clever boy.

That will serve you well—if you live long enough."

Gemma's jaw clenched.

She forced herself to meet his gaze. "You don't scare us."

"Oh, I should hope not," Weiss said softly. "Fear clouds judgment. I need you sharp."

He turned forward again, speaking more to himself than to them. "Teenagers. Always so certain the world will bend to their will. You'll find the world is less forgiving than you imagine."

The road curved, headlights sweeping across an old farmhouse. Weiss's reflection flickered in the window beside Gemma, pale and ghostly.

She gripped the door handle, wishing with all her strength that Jack would come roaring over the fields on his dirt bike, reckless and grinning, ready to tear them out of the unknown soldiers hands.

But Jack wasn't here.

She and Chris were alone, in the belly of the Dark Wing.

And Agent Weiss had only just begun.

Chapter 12
The Facility

The convoy rolled off the county road and onto a stretch of cracked asphalt flanked by chain-link fences. A guard tower rose in the distance, its floodlights sweeping the perimeter. Beyond that, hidden among the darkened hills, a squat concrete complex crouched like a bunker.

The SUV braked at a gate. Steel bars slid open with a mechanical groan. Inside, soldiers in black uniforms moved with disciplined silence, weapons at the ready. No insignias. No flags. No names. Just the emblem on their shoulders: a black wing, outstretched.

Gemma's chest tightened. Chris's knee bounced restlessly beside her.

The vehicle stopped at a loading bay. Doors opened in unison, agents pulling the teens out with brisk, impersonal force. "Move," one barked.

Cold fluorescent light flooded their eyes as they were marched down a sterile corridor of smooth concrete and steel doors. The sound of their sneakers squeaked against the polished floor. Every few feet, security cameras followed their movement, lenses twitching.

Agent Weiss walked ahead, hands folded behind his back, as though leading a tour. "Welcome," he said, "to one of our less… public facilities. You may consider it a safe house, though safety is relative, of course."

Gemma glared. "Where are you taking us?"

"To answers," Weiss replied smoothly. "Yours and mine."

They reached a reinforced door. A keypad flashed. Weiss pressed his palm against a scanner. With a hiss of hydraulics, the door opened into a laboratory.

It was bright, antiseptic. Stainless steel counters lined with instruments. Tanks of pale fluid, suspended with shapes just indistinct enough to be unsettling. Monitors displaying unfamiliar genetic code, scrolling endlessly.

At the center stood Dr. Blackburn. A man in his late sixties, silver hair cropped short, lab coat pristine. His sharp features softened only by the curiosity in his eyes— curiosity like a scalpel's edge.

"Ah," Blackburn said, removing a pair of latex gloves with practiced ease. "These are the witnesses?"

"Friends of the subject," Weiss corrected.

"They saw him... change."

Blackburn's eyes flicked over the two teens, studying them with the same detached interest he might show a specimen on a slide. "Fascinating."

Chris's voice cracked, but he forced it steady. "We're not saying anything. You can't make us."

Blackburn's lips curved into something that wasn't quite a smile. "Oh, you'd be surprised what the human mind reveals under the right conditions."

Gemma's heart pounded as Weiss gestured for the agents to seat them at a bolted steel table.

The fluorescent lights hummed overhead. The air stank of disinfectant and ozone.

For the first time, Gemma realized they weren't just prisoners. They were experiments waiting to begin.

Chapter 13
The Hunt Begins

The barn doors slammed open with a metallic shriek.

Jack tore out into the night on his dirt bike, the engine's roar deeper, louder, almost animal. The machine no longer looked cobbled together—it gleamed with slick black plating that rippled as if alive, faint blue light pulsing through its frame like veins. Armor stretched over the wheels, the handlebars, the engine block. It wasn't just his bike anymore. It was something new, something built for war.

And so was he.

Broken1's voice murmured in his ear, threaded through the hum of the engine. "I have integrated with your vehicle. The tracks of the Dark Wing convoy are clear. We can catch them."

Wind ripped at Jack's face as the helmet sealed tight around his head.

His vision sharpened—Broken1 overlaying glowing trails across the ground ahead, tire marks that blazed bright against the dark road.

"They're not getting away," Jack growled, twisting the throttle.

The bike surged forward, unnatural speed kicking dirt and gravel behind them. Fences blurred past. The stars wheeled above. Jack leaned into every curve with perfect instinct, the machine and rider fused into one.

For the first time since the crater, he felt power burning through him—not the hollow ache of loss, but fire. Purpose.

"Gemma. Chris. Hold on."

The fluorescent lights in the facility buzzed like angry bees.

Gemma and Chris sat rigid at the steel table, two agents looming behind them. Weiss stood at ease by the wall, jacket unbuttoned, his gaze sharp and patient. Dr. Blackburn busied himself with a tray of instruments, glass vials catching the light like icy teeth.

Gemma's wrists ached from the cold metal restraints clamped around them. Chris sat beside her, stiff with fury, his glasses sliding down the bridge of his nose.

Blackburn turned, syringe in hand. "We'll start simple," he said, his tone almost cheerful. "Just a blood draw. Nothing invasive—yet."

Gemma's pulse hammered. She tugged against the cuffs. "You can't do this! We didn't do anything!"

Weiss's voice slid through the room, calm as ever. "You did the one thing you shouldn't have... You saw. Wrong place at the wrong time. Pity."

He stepped closer, resting his hands lightly on the back of Chris's chair. "And I need to know just how much he told you before we collect what we want from all of you."

Chris's jaw clenched. He said nothing. Blackburn smiled faintly, tapping the syringe to clear the air bubbles. "Brave," he said. "Bravery makes excellent data."

The needle glinted under the light.

And far above the hills, cutting across the back roads in a blaze of blue, Jack was coming.

Chapter 14
Specter

The dirt bike screamed down the back roads, its tires glowing faintly against the cracked asphalt. Blue light pulsed through the black armor sheathing the frame, through Jack's gauntlets, through the veins of the helmet clamped around his head. The world blurred past in streaks of shadow and starlight.

Jack's voice cut through the roar of the engine. "Who were they? The men who took Gemma and Chris?"

Broken1's voice answered from the helmet, calm, resonant. "They are called the Dark Wing.

A covert military syndicate. They exist outside normal command structures, answerable only to their highest officers. Their purpose is singular: containment and weaponization of recovered extraterrestrial technology...

The man leading them, is known to the Core's data library as Agent Weiss. He is extremely dangerous. We have no other data."

Jack's grip on the handlebars tightened. "So they've been waiting for me?"

"They have been waiting for anyone like you," Broken1 said. "For decades they have hunted fragments, ruins, signals. You are the first living success thus far. They will not let you go."

Jack's jaw clenched. He leaned harder on the throttle, the bike howling like a living thing. "Then I'll tear them apart!"

Broken1's voice was quiet, but sharp. "Not without discipline."

Headlights flared ahead. A semi-truck lurched out from a side road, its massive grill filling the lane. There was no time. No gap to swerve through.

Jack's breath caught.

"Hold on," Broken1 said.

The world bent.

For a heartbeat, Jack felt his body unravel —like his skin had become static, his bones liquid.

Cold rushed through him, and the sound of the truck was inside his skull, vibrating his teeth. The headlights swallowed him ——and then they were past, the semi roaring into the distance, the bike solid again on the far side of the cab.

Jack gasped, almost losing control, the machine weaving before he righted it. His stomach twisted violently, his vision swimming.

"What the hell was that?!"

"Phase transition," Broken1 explained. "Matter displacement through quantum distortion. The Core grants you passage through solid objects for a few seconds."

Jack coughed, bile rising in his throat. His whole body tingled, every hair standing on end. "It felt like I was... inside that thing. Like it was inside me."

"You were," Broken1 said simply. "It is not pleasant. But it is survival."

Jack steadied the bike, adrenaline spiking as the road opened before him again. His lips curled into a shaky grin despite himself. "That was insane."

A pause, then: "Do not grow reckless," Broken1 warned.

Jack's grin faded, but the fire in his chest only burned hotter.

"They've got my family," he muttered. "Whatever it takes, I'm getting them back."

The road stretched on, glowing tire tracks guiding them toward the facility where his friends waited.

And this time, Jack swore, he wouldn't be too late.

Chapter 15
Breakout

The restraints bit into Gemma's wrists as Dr. Blackburn adjusted the straps, his movements precise, unhurried. The tray beside him gleamed with needles, scalpels, and tools she didn't recognize.

Chris sat restrained across the table, pale but defiant, his eyes locked on Weiss, who leaned casually in the corner, watching like a man studying theater.

"You should be proud," Blackburn murmured, selecting a syringe and holding it up to the light. "Few people contribute so directly to history. Your pain will teach us how to control him."

Gemma's stomach turned. "Jack will come for us," she spat.

Weiss tilted his head, amused. "I really hope that he does."

The fluorescent lights buzzed overhead, steady and merciless.

And then the alarm shrieked.

Red strobes lit the walls, bathing the lab in pulses of warning. Blackburn froze, syringe hovering mid-air. Weiss straightened, a flicker of irritation breaking his calm.

The wall to their right rippled. Like water disturbed by a stone, the concrete bulged inward, then split wide as Jack and his armored bike phased clean through.

The floor cracked beneath the tires as he skidded to a stop, blue light spilling from his gauntlets.

"Get away from them!" Jack roared.

Before the agents could draw, pulses of energy blasted from his hands— concussive bursts of light that slammed into their chests, hurling them against the walls. Blackburn staggered back, eyes wide in disbelief. Weiss's smile finally faltered.

Wild nano tendrils lashed out from Jack's armor, fluid and sharp, wrapping the restraints and ripping them apart with a metallic screech.

Gemma and Chris stumbled free. Chris grabbed his backpack from Weiss's feet. Gemma threw her arms around Jack hugging him, and Chris clinging to his shoulder.

For a moment, in the chaos and red strobe lights, they were just kids again, terrified but together.

The door burst open. A squad of guards

stormed in, sub-machine guns spitting fire. Gemma screamed as the air filled with the deafening chatter of bullets and smoke—
—Broken1's armor reacts instantly.

Black tendrils snapped outward, wrapping her and Chris in living plating. Blue light flared across their bodies as a shell of nanotech sealed over their skin. Bullets ricocheted and splintered harmlessly off the black surface, sparking as they struck. Gemma stared in shock, touching the alien plating on her chest. "Jack—what is this?"

Broken1's voice thundered through all their helmets at once:
"What I am about to do, I can only do once. Brace yourselves."

The armor brightened like cindering fire— blinding, brilliant blue flooding the room. Weiss shielded his eyes. Blackburn ducked behind the table. The guards froze in horror as the light reached its peak.

And then, with a sound like the universe itself snapping, Jack, Gemma, and Chris vanished in a pulse of pure radiance.

The lab was left in silence, smoke curling from the walls, restraints hanging broken, and nothing but the faint crackle of alien energy where the three had stood.

Chapter 16
Ashes of the Caretaker

The light burned out, leaving silence. Cold silence, and the strange hum of alien air.

Jack gasped, collapsing to his knees on smooth black flooring. His stomach lurched, his skin buzzing as if every atom of him had been ripped apart and stitched back together.

Chris retched beside him, bracing against a wall that curved seamlessly into ceiling. Gemma fell onto her hands and knees, coughing hard, eyes wild.

Then the floor shivered. A shape writhed and pooled behind them. Broken1 reformed, cables untangling, light flickering along its surface. The construct swayed like a drunkard, voice thin and strained. "I… am sorry. The energy cost…"

The light in its tendrils dimmed, sputtered —then went out.

What remained sagged into a lifeless heap of black cables on the alien floor.

"Broken?" Jack scrambled forward. "No, no, no—don't do this!"

He shoved at the limp mass, as if shaking it awake. Nothing. No voice in his head. No glow in the tendrils. Only silence.

Panic clawed up Jack's throat. He grabbed Chris by the shoulder. "Help me! We've got to get her to the med-bay. Where I woke up before."

Chris blinked, pale and disoriented, but nodded. Together they lifted the heavy, limp weight, Jack straining as the cables dragged against the slick floor. The corridors pulsed faintly with blue light, guiding them like veins through a body.

Jack didn't care how strange it was—he just followed his memory, dragging his dying—or dead—guardian toward salvation.

They reached the chamber with the floating slab. Jack hauled Broken1 onto it, the black mass spreading across the surface like a spilled shadow.

"Come on," Jack panted, chest heaving. "Don't you quit on me." He looked at Chris, desperation sharp in his eyes. "You're the genius—do something!"

Chris swallowed, staring at the walls where alien glyphs pulsed faintly, unfamiliar devices embedded seamlessly into the surface. "Jack, I don't even know where to start—"

"Try!" Jack's voice cracked. "Please."

Chris hesitated, then stumbled to a nearby

console, running his hands over the smooth, alien surface, searching for anything—buttons, switches, something.

Meanwhile, Gemma had wandered into the vast control room. Her knees went weak as she approached the enormous view port that stretched across the wall. Beyond it, the Earth hung in silence—blue, green, and white suspended in a black ocean.

Her breath caught. For the first time, the reality of it crashed over her: they weren't in Kansas anymore.

They weren't even on Earth.

But then she saw something else.

A speck. Tiny, fiery, rising through the atmosphere like a burning ember against the velvet dark. Slowly, steadily, it grew larger. Brighter.

Gemma's eyes widened. She pressed her hands to the glass. "Jack… Chris…" Her voice shook. "Something's coming."

They didn't hear her at first, still fumbling with glyphs and panels, voices overlapping in panicked argument.

"Jack!" she screamed this time, tearing her gaze from the growing fire to face them. Her eyes were wide, terrified. "Look!"

The burning speck was no longer small

and It was coming fast.

Chapter 17
Ghost Fire

The speck of fire grew into a streak. Then another. And another. Soon the night sky outside the view-port blazed with trails of flame, dozens of them cutting upward from Earth, their contrails fading in the thin blue atmosphere below.

Gemma's breath hitched. "M-Missiles... MISSILES!" she whispered.

Chris's face drained of color. "They're… they're firing at us."

Jack froze at the foot of the slab, Broken1's lifeless cables spilling over the edges. He turned toward the view-port, fists clenching, every muscle taut. There was no time. No weapons. No way to fight back.

The missiles rose higher, engines burning hot and furious. The cluster fanned out, arcing straight toward the Aegis.

The streaks of fire filled the view-port, multiplying until it felt as if the entire world had launched its fury into orbit.

"Jack…" Gemma's voice broke. She pressed her back against the wall as if trying to shrink away from the impossible storm rushing toward them.

The first warhead struck.

The control room filled with blinding white light—then the missile… passed through. Not shattered. Not deflected. It simply phased into ghostly transparency, dissolving through the floor beneath their feet and vanishing out the other side of the ship.

Jack stumbled back, blinking furiously. "What the hell—"

Another missile followed. Then ten. Then twenty. Each one tore through the ship like a phantom, their fiery trails cutting through the alien control room, through consoles, through the slab itself. The friends flinched as warheads phased inches from their faces, their ghostly roars filling the chamber, their bodies untouched.

One by one, the storm of fire bled through the Aegis, harmless, powerless, and carried helplessly into the abyss beyond. Then silence.

Gemma lowered her hands, shaking, eyes wide. "We… we should be dead."

Chris swallowed hard, adjusting his glasses with trembling fingers. "Some kind of hologram?!..No. No—something's protecting us. Some kind of… dimensional shielding?"

Jack stared at the black pile of the lifeless alien remains on the slab, jaw tight. Whatever this ship was, it wasn't as powerless as Broken1 had made it sound.

Command Center
Dark Wing

The war room smelled of steel and recycled air, humming with the constant pulse of electronics.

Monitors lined the walls, each one showing telemetry of the missile barrage, then the impossible result reported: ZERO IMPACT.

General Mason stood rigid at the head of the table, arms clasped behind his back. His face was weathered, cut deep with lines of a long command and practiced cruelty.

His gaze stayed locked on the central screen as the missiles passed uselessly through the alien vessel and drifted out into space, dying embers against the void.

At his side, Agent Weiss remained still as stone, eyes fixed and thoughtful.

"Stand down," Mason ordered. His voice was gravel wrapped in steel. "No more launches."

One of the officers turned in disbelief. "But sir—"

"Do it," Mason snapped.

The officer paled and nodded, relaying the order. The room quieted, save for the hum of machines.

Mason finally turned his head toward Weiss. His eyes burned with fury, but his voice remained cold. "It still has power. More than we accounted for."

Weiss adjusted his gloves with calm precision. "Missiles are a waste, then."

"Correct." Mason's lip curled. "And waste is weakness. We won't waste again. The Aegis isn't just shielding itself. It's phasing attacks like our previous attempts. Our weapons are gnats against a giant."

Weiss's expression didn't change. "Then we adapt. Watch. Wait. And strike where it cannot defend."

Mason's jaw tightened. "The boy."

"Yes," Weiss said softly. "The boy is the weakness."

Chapter 18
The Shadow on the Ridge

Far below, in the desert shadows, hidden silos cracked open like metal jaws. Missiles screamed upward in a chorus of fire, their exhaust scorching the canyon walls before they curved toward the stars.

On the ridge above, a small figure crouched, her silhouette framed against the blaze of rocket ignition. Honiael watched with ancient narrowed eyes, her pale features lit by the inferno's glow. Her frame was short and lithe, her armor sleek and angular, shifting faintly as though alive.

An alien blade, curved and cruel, rested across her back; a pistol-like weapon, humming faintly with inner light, rode her hip.

Her lips curled. "Primitive. Loud. Wasteful."

She laughed softly, a musical sound swallowed by the desert wind.

Through her visor, she tracked the missiles screaming upward, chasing their prey like angry fireflies. And then—she saw the futility. Warheads turned to ghosts, sliding harmlessly through the ancient satellite like smoke through a dream.

She chuckled again, shaking her head.

"Predictable."

Then she touches a control on her wrist as a sleek helmet builds around her head and long pointed ears before vanishing like smoke.

The night swallowed her whole, her form dissolving into nothing. Only the faint shimmer of disturbed dust marked her passage as she descended the ridge and strode straight toward the silo base.

Guards patrolled, rifles gleaming under the floodlights. One paused, frowning, his breath fogging in the chill night. A whisper of motion brushed past his ear.

He turned sharply, weapon raised. Nothing.

Another guard felt the tug of fingers on his belt, spun, and swore.

His radio crackled, but he found only the empty night.

Honiael moved unseen among them, a phantom wrapped in stealth. Each step precise. Each movement fluid. She slipped through the outer doors without a sound.

Dark Wing Command

The war room still hummed with subdued tension, the failed missile strike hanging like smoke. General Mason leaned over the central display, eyes narrowed at the readings. Weiss stood at his side, his voice low, measured, threading through the static of radio chatter.

"The Key," Weiss murmured. "If the boy has it—or if the Core guides him to it—it won't matter what arsenal we throw at him. The Aegis Core will awaken fully."

Mason grunted. "And if it does, then our window closes forever."

Weiss's gaze was calm, calculating. "We have leads. Fragments of transmissions. Patterns. The Key is not lost. Time cannot hide its beacon forever."

Mason straightened, his shadow stretching across the glowing table. "Then find it. I won't have this… alien relic sitting over our heads another day while Washington breathes down my neck."

Just then, the door hissed open. A young command officer hurried in, datapad clutched tight. He crossed the threshold in a rush—then stumbled violently, crashing to one knee. The datapad clattered across the floor.

"Sir—!" He looked behind him, bewildered, rubbing his shin as though he'd tripped on something. But the floor was bare. Empty. Weiss's eyes flicked briefly toward the door, his expression unreadable. Mason didn't notice, already barking for the report.

The officer scrambled to his feet, breathless.

"Telemetry analysis, Sir. The… the Key's signal, we think we've triangulated its possible location—"

He retrieved the pad, tapping frantically as Mason snatched it from his hands. Weiss leaned in, eyes narrowing at the data on the screen.

Behind them, unseen, the faint shimmer of air shifted near the corner of the room. Invisible fingers brushed the wall as Honiael listened, her smile hidden.

Chapter 19
Threads in the Dark

General Mason studied the datapad with the intensity of a predator scenting blood. The command center buzzed quietly, men and women at their stations, screens flickering with telemetry and satellite relays.

Weiss remained poised at his side, his hands folded neatly behind his back. "The triangulation points us to one of two possible sites. Both… inconvenient. Our teams will narrow down the best possibility with a little more time."

"Exotic is the word," Mason muttered. He jabbed the screen with a thick finger. "Deep under the ice shelf in Greenland—or in the middle of the goddamn Amazon."

"Two places the public cannot simply wander," Weiss said softly. "Two places where Dark Wing can operate without oversight."

Mason's jaw tightened. "Then we hit both. Split teams. If the Key is at either site, we'll bring it back. If not, we burn the site clean and move south."

Weiss's lips curved faintly, though it was not quite a smile. "Efficient. Decisive.

But…" His eyes flicked to the view port, where the Aegis Core still loomed in orbit. "None of this matters if the boy unlocks the Core before we reach it."

Mason exhaled through his nose like a bull. "Agent Weiss, your team will investigate the Jungle. Make preparations."

Neither man noticed the shimmer in the corner of the room—the way the air bent faintly, as though someone leaned casually against the wall, listening. Honiael's invisible grin widened at every word.

Aegis Core – Medbay

Broken1 lay across the alien slab like a fallen puppet, cables limp, his once-writhing form reduced to silence. Jack knelt at his side, one hand gripping the cool black plating as though he could will life back into it.

"Come on," Jack pleaded, voice raw. "You've saved me twice now—don't stop here. Don't leave us."

Gemma pressed close, resting a trembling hand on Jack's shoulder. Her eyes were wide and wet, flicking between him and the inert machine. "Jack… she doesn't look like she's coming back."

Chris shifted uneasily, trying to swallow the lump in his throat. He'd seen plenty of machines die, from fried motherboards to shorted-out consoles. This was different. This wasn't a machine. Not to Jack. Not to any of them anymore.

"We have to do something," Jack insisted. He grabbed Chris's sleeve. "You're the genius here! You always figure stuff out. Fix him!"

Chris shook his head, his voice cracking. "I can't! I don't even know how she works. I don't even think she's... meant to be fixed like a normal system."

Jack's jaw clenched, his eyes burning with desperation. "She was the only one who knew how this ship works. He's the only one who knew why I'm even here. Without her, we're—" His voice broke. "We're screwed."

A faint shudder rippled through Broken1's body, then a sickening stillness. Her frame began to unravel, cables curling and flaking into ash-like particles.

The three of them watched helplessly as the black lattice of his form collapsed piece by piece, revealing a hard, crystalline core.

"No!" Jack's shout echoed off the med-bay

walls. He pounded the slab with his fist, the sound hollow and final.

Within seconds, the rest of Broken1 disintegrated into dust. What remained on the slab was a single black, diamond-shaped device, smooth as glass, pulsing weakly with a single blue light.

Gemma covered her mouth with a hand, her tears slipping free. Chris reached forward with trembling fingers, stopping short of touching it.

Jack stared down at the blinking shard, chest heaving. To him it looked like the last heartbeat of a dying friend.

Chapter 20
The Silence Between Stars

The days bled into each other aboard the Aegis Core.

Jack, Gemma, and Chris drifted through the vast corridors like ghosts, the ship humming faintly beneath their feet but offering no guidance, no answers. The absence of Broken1 was more than just a silence — it was a void, a suffocating weight that pressed in on them from every black, alien wall.

The first night they had huddled together in the control room, staring down at the Earth turning silently below. So close, so impossibly far.

By the third day, the last of Chris's protein bars had been split into careful halves. Their two bottles of water dwindled, rationed to desperate sips.

Jack leaned against the wall, head tipped back, throat burning with thirst.

His eyes locked on one of the translucent blue slugs as it slimed lazily across the smooth floor, its faint blue glow trailing like a comet's tail. He nudged it with his boot. The slug farts nervously.

Jack smirked weakly, though his voice

came out rasping and thin. "I swear, if I get any hungrier, I'm eating one of these things."

Gemma gave him a tired glare. "Don't even joke about that."

"I'm not joking," Jack muttered, watching the slug wobble away.

The silence stretched again. Chris sat cross-legged on the control room floor, his laptop resting on his knees. He hadn't planned to open it — it was instinct, a muscle memory, something to fill the endless hours. He pressed the power button almost without thinking.

The familiar chime made all three of them look up. For a moment, the normal glow of the startup screen felt like a piece of home. Then the screen flickered.

Once. Twice.

The glow shifted to a harsh crimson. An alarm-like pulse filled the screen, flashing red in rhythm with the pounding of their hearts.

"Chris...?" Gemma whispered.

"I didn't—" Chris stammered, jerking his hands back.

Before any of them could move, the floor beneath Chris rippled like liquid. Black cables erupted upward, writhing and snapping around the laptop like living snakes. They swallowed the device whole, the screen going dead-black before sparking back to life.

Jack shoved Chris backward, his own heart hammering in his ears. "Get away from it!"

The three huddled as the laptop trembled in its cocoon of cables, the glow building until words crawled across the screen in jagged blue light:

JACK HELP ME

Then again.

JACK HELP ME

Over and over, the message burned into their retinas, each repetition more frantic than the last.

Jack stared at the screen, his stomach twisting. His voice came out hoarse, almost unbelieving.

"…Broken1?"

Chapter 21
The Voice of the Ship

Jack's pulse hammered in his ears as he edged toward the laptop. The blue words still burned across the screen, desperate, insistent.

JACK HELP ME.

Then, without warning, the screen glitched, flickered—

And a cartoon rabbit's lopsided grin appeared in grainy black and white.

Jack froze, staring as the rabbit leaned with his carrot, chomping with casual indifference. "Eh, whazzup, doc?"

"What the hell..." Jack muttered under his breath.

Chris blinked. "That's—cartoons? From the forties?"

The cartoon looped once, then flickered away. The laptop spasmed with static.

Then, as if something had burst awake, the entire control room came alive.

One by one, the black walls bloomed with light. Screens they hadn't even realized were embedded in the surfaces snapped to life.

Holographic projections spilled out of the air like ghosts—television broadcasts, old movies, fragments of newsreels, sitcoms, even grainy home footage. The air vibrated with a dizzying chorus of sound: laughter tracks, gunfire, music, applause.

Gemma gasped, her hands flying to her mouth. "It's… it's Earth. It's all of Earth."

Every surface around them seemed drenched in human history. Jack spun slowly in place, his eyes wide, as the flood of imagery washed over him.

The laptop beeped, drawing their attention back. New words scrolled across the screen, this time steadier, deliberate.

I AM THE AEGIS CORE.

I AM ALONE.

HELP ME, JACK.

Jack's face lit with a hope he hadn't felt since Broken1 collapsed. He turned toward Gemma and Chris, almost laughing with relief.

"It's the ship! The whole ship's alive!"

Chris's brow furrowed, eyes darting between the flickering holograms. "Alive… or mad."

Jack ignored him, leaning close to the laptop. "Okay! Okay—you want me to help? Tell me how.

We need water. Food. My friends are starving. How do we—how do we fix

Broken1?"

The words appeared quickly now, sharp and clear:

PUT BROKEN1'S CORE INTO THE GENERATOR.

Jack looked down at the diamond-shaped shard still clutched in his hand. The faint blue light pulsed, as if hearing.

"What generator!?" he demanded, almost shouting at the screen.

The response was immediate:

FOLLOW THE HALLWAY.

Jack leapt to his feet, adrenaline surging through his veins.

"That's it—that's all we need! Come on!" He held up the glowing shard triumphantly. "We can bring her back!"

Gemma and Chris exchanged a nervous glance. The walls were still alive with fractured pieces of Earth's history—flashes of laughter and gunshots, oceans and skylines, all bleeding together into a dizzying storm.

But Jack didn't notice. His eyes blazed with renewed fire as he sprinted toward the corridor, the pulsing black diamond clutched in his fist like a beacon.

Chapter 22
Hunter and Prey

The Dark Wing base had settled into its usual rhythm: the low murmur of comms chatter, the faint hum of generators echoing through the steel corridors. Most of the agents had retired to their bunks, but one figure still moved with quiet precision. Agent Weiss.

He walked with the same disciplined calm he always carried, his coat draped neatly over one arm as he made his way toward his quarters. To the guards and staff who saw him, he was nothing unusual—just a man ending a long day.

But in the shadows, a second presence stalked him. Honiael's slender form slipped invisibly along the wall, her steps noiseless, her laughter silent in her throat. Her blade and energy pistol hung at her hips, unseen.

The human commander and his men were children fumbling with stolen toys, she thinks. She slips by him through the sliding door and into his quarters.

Weiss closed the door behind him, unbuttoning his shirt with a sigh. He moved with deliberate ease, setting his sidearm on the dresser, folding his clothes with mechanical neatness. To any observer, he was vulnerable, unguarded.

Honiael smirked, invisible and patient.

Then Weiss reached into his nightstand. His fingers closed around a sleek device, no larger than a pistol grip, its surface humming with faint red light. Without hesitation, he pivoted, pointing directly at the empty air where she stood.

The device cracked with a sharp electrical pop. A wave of energy splashed against her cloaked form, tearing her invisibility apart like shattering glass.

Honiael's eyes widened. "—What!—?"

The second crack dropped her to the floor, spasming as the current surged through her body. She clawed for her weapon, but her muscles betrayed her, seizing against the current. Darkness swallowed her before her fingers could touch the hilt.

She awoke groggily, her head lolling forward. The cold bite of steel pressed against her wrists and ankles. Honiael blinked until her vision cleared, only to realize her situation: stripped to a thin undergarment, bound tightly to a steel chair, every elegant limb pinned.

Her long blonde hair clung to her damp

face, her pointed ears twitching with fury.

A sharp sting snapped her back to full awareness. Weiss stood before her, his gloved hand lowered from the slap, his expression calm as ever. He pulled another chair close and sat down across from her, perfectly composed.

"Welcome back," he said smoothly. "I trust the accommodations are… humbling."

Honiael glared, baring her teeth. "You— how?"

Weiss's lips twitched, almost into a smile. He tapped his eye with one finger. The faintest glimmer caught the light—a shimmer across the iris that wasn't human.

"You're not the first of your kind I've met," he said, his tone conversational. "Your people have been slipping in and out of this world for millions of years, thinking yourselves clever. We've been watching. Studying. Taking what we need."

He leaned forward with a sigh, his voice to a whisper. "These lenses? A trophy from one of your fallen. Recovered tech. You thought you were invisible." His smile sharpened. "You were never invisible to me."

Honiael's breath came fast, anger mixing with the faintest thread of unease. For the first time in a long while, she felt like the pray.

Chapter 23
The Price of Blood

The three friends moved cautiously through the alien corridor, their footsteps echoing on the black, seamless floors. The walls seemed to breathe around them, shifting in ways none of them wanted to acknowledge.

Jack slowed, running his fingers along the surface. "I swear this hallway wasn't here before. It's like the place rearranges itself every time we move."

Chris adjusted his glasses nervously. "Adaptive architecture. It's… alive enough to decide where it wants us to go."

"Yeah, well, I'd appreciate a straight hallway for once," Jack muttered.

A door shaped into existence ahead of them, smooth and featureless until a faint outline carved itself across the surface.

It parted silently, revealing a cavernous chamber beyond.

Gemma gasped. "It's a lab…"

The room spread out in a dizzying array of alien technology. Tubes and consoles stretched into the shadows above, glowing faintly with power. Transparent tanks, empty but glistening with fluid, lined the walls like forgotten coffins. In the center, a wide console pulsed awake as they stepped closer.

Behind them, Chris's laptop slithered down the corridor on a nest of writhing cables, following like a loyal pet. It skittered to a stop on the console, screen lighting with a flare of blue.

A pedestal rose from the floor, shifting and shaping itself until it formed a perfect cradle for the black diamond shard Jack carried.

Jack hesitated, then placed the object into it.

The console came alive. Light bled through the chamber in complex patterns, words flashing across the laptop's screen in steady, cold rhythm.

ORGANIC FLESH MUST BE USED TO CULTURE THE PROTEIN NANITES.

Jack blinked at it, stunned. "Wait. What?"

The text shifted.

INSERT HAND FOR REMOVAL.
I'M SORRY. IT'S THE ONLY WAY.

Gemma's eyes widened, her face pale. "Removal? What the hell does that mean?"

Jack turned toward the screen, voice rising with desperation. "What do you mean *removal*?! Removal of *what*?!"

The answer came at once:

IT IS THE ONLY WAY TO CHARGE THE NANITES NECESSARY TO REMAKE BROKEN1.

A suffocating silence filled the lab.

Jack looks down at his hand, his fingers trembling. He swallows hard, a knot twisting in his stomach.

Chapter 24
The Sacrifice

The chamber hummed with an unnatural rhythm, the console pulsing with blue light as if it could hear their very breaths. Jack stared at the opening that had appeared on its surface, the edges lined with faint, shimmering light. It seemed to wait for him, hungry.

"I have to do it," Jack said at last, his voice low but firm. "Broken1's the only one who knows how to work this ship. Without her, we're stranded. Dead. This is the only way."

Chris's face twisted. "No. Jack, listen to yourself—this thing is asking you to *feed it your hand.* You don't even know what it's going to do. What if it takes more? What if it kills you outright?"

"It's worth it," Jack snapped, his frustration boiling over. "Without Broken1, we don't have food, we don't have water—we don't even know how to escape this thing! We'll starve to death drifting above Earth or until Dark Wing hunts us down. I'm not letting that happen!"

Gemma's eyes darted between them, her hands trembling. "Jack, There has to be another way—"

"There isn't!" Jack shouted, his voice raw. He turned toward the console, jaw clenched. "I'm doing it."

He raised his hand, fingers curling into a fist, and took a step forward.

But before he could thrust it into the opening, Chris's hand shot out, gripping Jack's wrist like iron.

"Chris, what are you—"

With a guttural cry, Chris yanked Jack back and shoved his own arm forward. His hand plunged into the opening before Jack could stop him.

A hiss filled the chamber, sharp and metallic. A lance of light seared out of the console. Chris screamed, his whole body convulsing as the chamber filled with the acrid stench of burning flesh.

Gemma shrieked. Jack lunged forward, too late, grabbing Chris by the shoulders as the boy tore his arm free. Chris collapsed to his knees, gasping and shaking. His wrist—ended in a smooth, cauterized stump, the wound sealed perfectly shut by the alien laser.

"Chris!" Gemma fell beside him, tears streaming down her cheeks as she tried to steady him. "Oh God, oh God—"

Jack's chest heaved, his vision swimming with horror. He cupped Chris's face, forcing him to meet his eyes. "Why would you— why the hell would you do that?!"

Chris's teeth chattered as he fought for breath. "Because… I love you. I couldn't let you do it. Don't make me regret it!"

Jack's throat tightened. He wanted to scream at him, to call him an idiot, but the words refused to come.

Behind them, the console roared to life. Tendrils of black light surged outward, weaving themselves into form. The diamond shard pulsed violently, then dissolved into the twisting strands. Cables whipped together, thickening, reshaping.

The three of them stared in awe through their grief as the cables coiled into a humanoid form, writhing and solidifying until a new figure stood before them. Taller, sharper, more angular than before, the surface gleamed like obsidian streaked with blue fire.

Where Broken1 had seemed ancient, disjointed, fragile—this was something new. Something stronger.

Gemma whispered the thought none of them dared to say aloud.

"…Broken1?"

Chapter 25
The Mother's Hand

The figure that emerged from the console shifted, its black form glimmering with rivers of blue light. For a long breath, Jack, Gemma, and Chris just stared, unsure if this was their ally reborn—or some new horror.

Then the shape leaned forward, the lines of its face smoothing into something almost kind. Its voice came, soft and melodic this time, carrying a warmth that tugged at their hearts.

"Jack. Gemma. Christopher."

Jack blinked. "You... you sound different."

"I am still Broken," the voice replied, her tone full of gentle assurance. "But I am more. I am whole. You may call me... Broken2, if that pleases you."

Chris managed a strained laugh through his pain. "She... she sounds like my mom when I was sick."

Broken2 knelt before him, her glowing eyes studying his as if she could see the pain and sacrifice etched into his soul. Her voice lowered, almost a whisper.

"Brave Christopher. You gave of yourself to bring me back. I will not let you remain broken."

She extended a hand, drawing them toward another structure rising from the floor—a machine that pulsed with a faint, heartbeat-like rhythm.

Jack tightened his grip on Chris's shoulder. "Wait—what are you going to do to him?"

Broken2's head tilted, almost in reproach. "Mend what was lost."

Gemma swallowed hard. "But how—?"

Before anyone could stop her, Broken2 gently but firmly guided Chris's severed wrist onto the machine's surface. Metal tendrils like silver hair snapped awake, wrapping around his arm.

Chris's eyes went wide. "W-wait, hold on —"

The machine hissed, and a hundred needle-thin micro-tendrils stabbed into his skin.

Chris screamed in agony, the sound echoing down the vast chamber. His body arched as the device worked furiously, nanites crawling into his veins like fire.

"Make it stop!" Gemma cried, tears streaming as she clutched Jack's arm.

But Jack shook his head, his gut wrenching. "No… look—look at his arm!"

Through Chris's sobs, they saw it—shimmering strands weaving across the cauterized stump, flesh re-knitting in patterns of silver and black. Bone took shape first, latticed with alien steel.

Muscle and sinew followed, then skin, pale but flecked with tiny black motes of nanites.

Finally, fingers unfurled like petals, trembling, then curling into a fist.

The tendrils withdrew. Chris collapsed forward, gasping, staring at his own hand—his *new* hand. It looked human, save for faint lines of blue light running under the skin like veins of starlight.

Gemma pressed a hand to her mouth, her eyes wide in disbelief. "Chris, your hand… it's rebuilt."

Broken2 touched Chris's shoulder, her voice soft as a mother's lullaby. "No, child. *We rebuilt you.* The Aegis Core and I—together. You are part of us now."

Chris flexed his glowing fingers, staring between Jack and Gemma, terror and awe warring in his expression.

Jack swallowed hard, his heart hammering. For the first time since they'd been taken aboard, he felt something like hope.

Chapter 26
Flesh and Steel

Chris sat slumped against the machine, his chest heaving, his eyes fixed on the arm that hadn't existed a minute before.

His new hand trembled as he lifted it into the light—smooth, pale skin stretched over tendons that pulsed faintly with a glow from beneath. The blue veins flickered like stars under ice.

He flexed his fingers slowly, one by one. A ghost of pain shivered through him, but the hand obeyed, strong and steady.

"It feels…" Chris's voice cracked, "…it feels like mine. But it's not, is it?"

Gemma knelt beside him, gently clasping his glowing hand. Her thumb brushed across the knuckles, warm against the strange coldness radiating from it. "It's still yours," she whispered. "Just… different."

"It's better then it was before." Broken2 hums wistfully.

Jack crouched across from them, restless energy coursing through him. He raked a hand through his messy hair, his face caught somewhere between awe and fear. "Chris your hand, Man!."

Chris's eyes flicked up sharply, wounded.

"You think I *wanted* this? I did it for *you,*
Jack! For all of us!" He gestured at
Broken2, who watched silently from the
shadows, her glowing eyes patient.

Jack sighed, guilt softening the edge of his
voice. "I know. I know, man. You saved us.
I just… I don't know what this means for
you now."

Chris let out a shaky laugh. "Neither do I.
But if it means I can play games better,
maybe it's worth it."

Gemma gave him a small smile through
her tears. "Nerd."

For a moment, the three of them sat there,
the silence filled with the hum of unseen
machinery and the faint, organic rhythm of
the ship.

Finally, Broken2 stepped forward, her
voice tender, like a mother soothing
frightened children. "You are afraid. That is
natural. But know this—nothing was taken
from Christopher that he did not choose to
give. He is still himself. And more than
himself."

Chris stared at his hand again, then
clenched it into a fist. "More than myself…"

Jack stood, pacing, trying to shake off the
dread tightening in his chest. "Okay, fine.
He's… rebuilt. But what about us? We still

don't have food, or water, or any way back to Earth."

Broken2's gaze followed him calmly. "Those things will come. For now, trust that the Aegis Core has given you what you need most: each other."

Her words hung in the air, heavy with meaning.

Jack stopped pacing, caught off guard. He glanced at Gemma, then at Chris, and for the first time since this nightmare began, he let himself breathe.

They were still together. That had to count for something.

Chapter 27
Shadows in the Chair

The laboratory was cold—too clean, too sharp. Every surface gleamed under the clinical white lights, but the smell of ozone and antiseptic couldn't mask the undertone of fear.

Honiael strained against her bonds, the chair biting into her wrists and ankles. The straps glowed faintly, alien in origin, humming with energy that burned her skin whenever she tried to move.

Her long, golden hair clung damply to her cheeks, sweat beading on her smooth, pale skin. The elegant points of her ears twitched involuntarily, betraying her agitation.

Across from her, Dr. Blackburn adjusted the dials of a head-mounted array of flashing lights, the machine's hum deepening. Syringes of iridescent liquid rested on a tray beside him, each one stranger than the last.

"You're resilient," the doctor murmured, almost with admiration. "Your species always was.

Neural resistance far higher than baseline human. But not infinite."

Honiael spat at his feet, her voice a venomous whisper. "You meddle with things you cannot begin to understand."

Agent Weiss leaned casually against a counter, his expression as calm as if he were overseeing a routine interrogation. His tie hung loose, his sleeves rolled up. "On the contrary," he said smoothly, "we understand quite a lot. Enough to know you've been hunting the same thing we are."

The doctor turned a knob. The head array bathed Honiael's face in strobing white light. She flinched, teeth clenched, but said nothing. The patterns shifted—slower now, almost hypnotic.

Blackburn slid a syringe into her arm. The liquid coursed through her veins like fire.

Her breath hitched, her body arching against the restraints.

Weiss stepped closer, his shadow falling across her. "Where is the Aegis Key?" he asked softly, his tone almost kind. "Tell me, and this ends."

Honiael squeezed her eyes shut, fighting it. Her kind had endured centuries of Dark Wing's crude interrogations. They had trained their minds, learned to resist.

But the flashing light gnawed at the edges

of her consciousness, fracturing her thoughts. The serum twisted her perceptions, dragging her into a half-dream, half-nightmare where the walls melted and voices whispered.

Her lips parted. Words slipped out before she could stop them. "The… the key… hidden… fragments… earth carries it still…"

Weiss leaned in, his voice silk and steel. "Where. Specifically."

She trembled, her eyes unfocused, her voice distant and broken. "The old city… stone buried deep… guarded by time and blood. The humans… they do not know what they hold…"

Her voice cracked into a cry as another surge of light pulsed across her vision.

Weiss smiled faintly, satisfied. He gave Blackburn a curt nod, and the doctor dialed the machine back just enough for her to slump in the chair, dazed but breathing. "Remarkable," Weiss said, straightening his jacket sleeve. "Even broken, she's beautiful. But now… she's useful."

Honiael's head lolled, her eyes glassy. For the first time since she'd entered the base, the predator looked like prey.

Chapter 28
The Tour

The straps hummed against Honiael's skin, every movement burning like live wire. She sat rigid in the interrogation chair, her long hair hanging damp against her face, her breath ragged from the drugs and light pulses that still echoed through her veins.

Agent Weiss crouched before her, one hand casually removing the head array, the other gripping her chin to lift her face toward his. His expression was calm, clinical, as if this were simply part of the job.

"You elves," he said softly, almost with admiration, "always think endurance is enough. But what's endurance against inevitability?" His eyes narrowed, the smile tugging at the corners of his mouth. "We know where the Key is now. A buried city, bristling with traps, sealed monsters, all waiting to be disturbed."

Honiael tried to turn her face away, but his grip was iron. Weiss leaned closer, voice dropping to a cruel whisper.

"You're going to spring every trap for us. You're going to slay every beast. You'll carve us a path to the Key with your pretty little hands. And when I hold it in mine—" he tilted her chin higher, his smile sharpening, "I may let you see it, just before I empty your filthy elven skull."

Honiael's breathing deepened, her violet eyes glowing suddenly, brilliantly. The light wasn't mere fury—it was *power*, spilling out in dazzling ripples, burning into Weiss's gaze like twin stars.

For an instant, the air in the lab seemed to thrum. Dr. Blackburn froze, transfixed. His mouth fell open as his hands trembled over his tray of syringes. "She's… beautiful," he whispered, his voice cracking with awe. "Perfect… I love her—"

Weiss chuckled low in his throat, utterly unfazed. He tapped his eye with one finger, and the iris flashed faintly, the delicate pattern of elven circuitry glinting in the light. "That's the weakness of your little tricks," he said, smiling as the glow from Honiael's eyes reflected off his lenses. "Psychic illusions. Parlor games for the weak-minded."

Blackburn staggered forward, his pupils blown wide, his face slack with desire. "No —don't you see? She's divine. She—she's *mine!*"

Weiss's smile flattened into mild annoyance. He gestured lazily with two fingers. "Get him out."

Two guards moved in swiftly, seizing the doctor by the arms. Blackburn screamed, kicking against the floor, his voice raw and desperate. "Don't take her from me! She's my everything—she's *everything!*"

The guards dragged him from the room, his cries fading into the corridor beyond.

Weiss exhaled smoke from a cigarette, the gray ribbon curling into Honiael's face. He gave her chin one last tug before releasing it.

"You almost had me," he said with mock admiration.

"Almost. But that's the thing about illusions —once you know the trick, they lose their power."

He took a slow drag and smiled around the cigarette. "We're going on a trip."

Honiael glared at him, her eyes still glowing faintly violet, but inside she seethed. Her spell hadn't broken him—but it had reached someone. And that, she thought darkly, was proof that he wasn't untouchable.

Chapter 29
School Is in Session

The ship's hum seemed softer now, almost like it was listening, as Jack, Chris, and Gem sat cross-legged on the smooth floor of the control room. Broken2 stood before them, her presence more mother than machine, her corded face illuminated by the fiery blue glow of the walls.

"Children," she said gently, "you must learn if you are to survive."

The air shimmered, and a lattice of light spun into being. Holograms bloomed above their heads—shapes, symbols, entire worlds stitched together from threads of light. The kids gasped in unison, their wide eyes reflecting the spectacle.

"First, your needs." Broken2 touched the wall. It rippled like liquid under her hand. A clear spout emerged, and crystalline water poured into a waiting basin.

Chris sprang to his feet. He pressed his palm nervously against the wall. Another stream appeared, and he cupped his hands to drink. His laugh was muffled by the gulping sound.

Jack let out a sigh of relief. "Okay. So... we won't die of thirst."

"Nor of hunger," Broken2 said. She guided them to a rounded console in the corner. "The constructor can fabricate food. Nutritionally complete, if not… luxurious."

A tray slid out holding three steaming bars. Jack tore off a bite and chewed, squinting. "Huh. Cardboard. But… like, good cardboard."

Chris snorted. "Better than slug stew." He nudged one of the pale slugs inching along the floor. It farted softly in protest, and he smirked.

Broken2 tilted her head and projected a hologram of the slugs, their translucent bodies mapped in glowing detail. "Do not mock them. The Volga slugs are essential. They consume toxins and excrete oxygen. You organics would suffocate without them."

The kids exchanged startled glances. Suddenly, the gassy little creatures didn't seem so ridiculous.

The holograms shifted again—this time to something vast. Galaxies spun. Stars flared and died. From the void emerged a colossal ship, so massive it looked like a continent drifting in space, its surface aglow with ancient symbols.

"This," Broken2 said reverently, "is the Aegis. My body. My memory. But know this: I am not whole."

The projections deepened. The Aegis under siege. Beams of energy slashing across its surface.

"My origin lies beyond this universe. The Aegis Core and her parent ship are over twenty-three billion years old, born from a universe that collapsed before this one. Who made us, and why—we no longer remember."

The images changed. Earth appeared—not the green-and-blue jewel they knew, but primordial and barren rock.

The Aegis floated above it, glowing as torrents of energy rained down. Seas swelled. Forests unfurled. The planet came alive.

"When the parent ship was attacked, it fled here.

The warp seizure that resulted nearly destroyed your solar system. I was detached, cast into orbit to stabilize. To repair. To seed. Refugees—beings not too different from yourselves—came aboard me, and for seven thousand years, they lived here as I Terra-formed the planet below."

Scenes unfolded of entire communities aboard the ship, different cultures blending, thriving in harmony with its living walls. "But time divides all peoples," Broken2 continued, her voice tinged with sorrow. "Most of the refugees eventually left me, descending to Terra to begin new civilizations, while the elites remained, claiming they alone were worthy to hold my secrets. They eventually fought within my halls for control of the Core."

The vision turned violent—elites in strange armor unleashing weapons, fire consuming the ship's grand chambers. Broken2's tone grew grave.

"We cast them out—forever exiled to the surface. But not before one of the last stole the Key and brought it to the surface below. The Key is not only the infinite power center of the Aegis… it is also our main library of knowledge. That likely contains the last hints of the parent ship's coordinates."

The final hologram flickered with the shape of a small black diamond, pulsing faintly with blue light—then dimmed, leaving only the silence of the control room.

Gemma hugged her knees, her face pale.

Chris stared at the empty air where the diamond had hovered. Jack looked between them, his throat tight.

Broken2 lowered herself to meet their eyes. "Without the Key, we are broken. Blind. But with it, we could be whole again. And only then will you stand a chance against what hunts you."

The three of them sat in silence, the immensity of the truth pressing down like a weight too vast to bear.

Finally Jack whispered, "Then we find it. We have to."

Broken2's expression softened, almost maternal. "Yes, Jack. We must."

Chapter 30
Iron Sharpens Iron

The room hummed as though alive, vast and echoing, with ceilings that seemed to stretch forever. Panels glowed faintly across the walls, bathing the floor in a steady blue light.

Jack, Chris, and Gem stood shoulder to shoulder, their footsteps lost in the immensity of the chamber.

"This is where you will sharpen yourselves,"

Broken2 said, her voice carrying with a weight both patient and commanding. "Iron sharpens iron. Alone you are fragile—but together, you may yet become strong."

She turned, her arms unfurling into long, shifting strands of black nanite cables that glimmered with blue veins of light. With delicate precision, she plucked three thick strands free, each writhing faintly as though alive.

She approached Gem first. "You have courage, though you doubt yourself. This will steady you."

The nanite strand slithered into Gemma's palm and curled around her wrist. It tightened, reshaping into a sleek gauntlet that pulsed softly with her heartbeat. Gem gasped as it seemed to breathe with her, an extension of her body.

Then Jack. Broken2 laid the second strand across his open hand. It spiraled upward like ivy, wrapping his forearm until it sealed with a hiss of blue light. Jack flexed his fist, and sparks of energy rippled across the gauntlet.

Finally Chris. Broken2 held the last coil in her palm. She studied him for a long moment, her gaze strangely soft. "I now sacrifice my hand," she said quietly. "For all of you. This is all that I can spare you. Take care of it."

The coil slid from her hand into his, coiling up his arm with surprising gentleness until it too sealed into a living gauntlet. Chris stared down at it, lips parted, then looked up at her, conflicted. "Why me?"

"Because knowledge without strength is wasted," Broken2 said. "And strength without knowledge is dangerous."

She raised her own arm, and her fingers unfolded into a fan of glowing glyphs. "Now, activate your environmental armor. The nanites will respond to your will."

The kids hesitated. Then, one by one, their bodies were swallowed by a cascade of black oil and scales, shifting and flowing like liquid metal until they stood clad in full suits of sleek armor. Blue light glowed at their joints and across their visors.

Jack looked down at himself, awe in his voice. "I look like a freaking superhero."

"Do not mistake appearance for mastery," Broken2 warned. "This armor grants you many abilities—strength to lift what you could not, speed to move like the wind, phasing to walk through obstacles, shields to repel harm, symbiosis to bond with machines, and a comm network linking you to one another… and to me."

The armor shifted slightly as she spoke, demonstrating: plates hardening, shields flickering, blue glyphs scrolling across their visors with data and readouts.

"Now—the weapons," Broken2 said.

She lifted her hand, and the nanites rippled into a blade. Then a shield. Then a spear. Then dissolved again into a plasma barrel. "Your mind will shape them. Focus your thought. Direct your form."

The hours that followed blurred into trials, exercises, and sudden challenges that tested their courage more than their strength. Sparks lit the room. The floor shifted beneath their feet. Strange targets appeared, only to vanish in bursts of light. Sometimes they laughed, sometimes they faltered, and sometimes they clung to one another, determined not to fail.

By the end, sweat clung to their foreheads and their hearts raced, but they stood taller, stronger.

Broken2 smiled. "You are ready for the beginning. Nothing more. Nothing less."

Soon the chamber echoed with their shouts and laughter, the air thick with smoke and ozone. For a brief moment, they weren't hunted kids or stranded survivors—they were adventurers. Heroes.

When the session finally ended, Broken2 dismissed the targets and guided them to a row of sealed doors.

"This ship will care for you," she said softly. "Each of you will have a place of your own."

The first door opened to Chris's quarters: a compact lab filled with glowing consoles, sleek benches, and his laptop resting neatly on the bed.

Chris froze, his throat catching.

"Your device is now part of me," Broken2 explained. "Through it, you have unrestricted access to the few databanks that remain. You can learn anything necessary to keep the Aegis Core alive."

Chris stepped inside, running his hands over the cool lab tables with a trembling reverence.

Next was Gemma's room. The door slid open to reveal soft pink walls, shelves of stuffed animals, and warm white lights. It looked like a childhood bedroom lifted from a dream.

Gem's hand went to her mouth. "This is… mine?"

"I designed it myself," Broken2 said, her voice almost tender.

Gem laughed, a sound equal parts disbelief and joy. Jack squeezed her hand. The kiss that followed was long, desperate, and aching—two young adults lost in the immensity of their fate, clinging to each other like a lifeline. Promises whispered in silence between their lips.

Finally, Broken2 led Jack to his room. Sleek and black, lined with faint blue tracery. A shower, a bed that seemed to hum faintly with energy.

Jack retracted his armor, and stepped into the strange shower, letting the hot water pound against his shoulders. For the first time in days, he felt clean, human.

When he finally lay trudged over and laid

back in the smooth bed, exhaustion pulled at him.

His eyes were half-lidded when the door whispered open.

Gemma stood there, smiling softly. She wore pale pink pajamas, her hair tumbling over her shoulders, her grin playful yet tinged with something more.

Jack blinked in surprise, then returned her smile.

She stepped inside, her gaze never leaving his, and the door shut quietly behind her.

Chapter 31
Shadows of Tomorrow

Chris sat cross-legged on the floor of his lab, the laptop warm against his thighs. He rubbed his tired eyes, but the scrolling code and fractured symbols on the screen kept tugging him forward.

He didn't even notice the hours slipping by, only the steady rhythm of his own heartbeat and the faint hum of the ship.

Most of the Aegis's databanks were locked, hidden behind access barriers that pulsed like living walls of light. But sometimes, if he pushed the right way, the walls shifted. And tonight, they shifted just enough to let him glimpse the truth.

The ship was dying. Power levels hovered at almost nothing—fractions of fractions of a percent, barely enough to keep lights on and air cycling. Chris frowned, muttering under his breath as he traced the energy readouts.

The Aegis wasn't a sleeping titan. It was a drifting corpse, one heartbeat away from silence. And the blueprints—the means to rebuild, to make anything—were sealed inside something called the Key.

He leaned closer to the screen as another

file cracked open, this one bearing the code-name: **Dark Wing**. He expected dossiers, weapons manifests, field reports. What he found instead chilled him: intercepted transmissions, fragmented voices speaking in hushed tones, their words soaked in something ancient and cruel.

He couldn't put his finger on it, only that the voices felt wrong, as if whatever controlled Dark Wing wasn't entirely human.

Chris swallowed, closing the file before his own imagination could eat him alive. But then, buried beneath strings of encrypted coordinates, a single point lit up on the map. A jungle basin, remote and green, circled in red.

His pulse quickened. Finally—a place to start looking for the Key.

Meanwhile, the ship slept around him. Down the hall, Jack and Gemma lay tangled together in the quiet glow of their quarters. For the first time in days, Gemma let herself drift.

Her dream began softly—warm sunlight, laughter, Jack's hand in hers. A world without fear. A world where she didn't have to be afraid of losing him.

But then the sky darkened. Shadows rippled across the earth, and something vast rose behind Jack, blotting out the light. A monster, a nightmare made flesh, its face lost in fire. She screamed his name, but he only smiled at her, pressed a kiss to her forehead, and shoved her away. She fell, reaching, as the flames swallowed him whole.

Her own scream yanked her awake. Gemma lay in the dark, trembling, her skin slick with sweat. Jack was still there, breathing steadily, his face calm in the dim light.

She pressed herself against him, clutching his shirt, whispering his name just to hear it spoken.

"It was just stress," she told herself. "Just stress. Just a dream."

But her heart wouldn't slow. And the fire still burned at the edges of her memory.

Chapter 32
Cargo

The floodlights on the tarmac painted the night in harsh white. Engines thundered as crews loaded crates of steel containers, weapons, and unmarked pallets into the yawning belly of a massive black C-5 Galaxy. Soldiers barked orders over the roar, straining against straps and levers.

In the middle of it all, strapped to a metal pallet like some grotesque offering, knelt Honiael. Her wrists and ankles were bound in steel cuffs, chains welded to the frame. A blindfold masked her glowing eyes, and a gag muffled her voice. Her silver-blonde hair spilled across her shoulders, catching the light like liquid fire.

She wore nothing but plain undergarments, stripped of armor, stripped of weapons, stripped of dignity.

Agent Weiss leaned against a Humvee as the troops heaved her pallet up the loading ramp. He exhaled smoke, the ember of his cigarette glowing red in the dark.

"Careful with that cargo, troops," he called, smirking. With a flick of his finger, he snapped the cigarette butt at her head. It bounced off her head with an explosion of cinders and fell into the shadows as he chuckled.

The engines rose to a roar, and soon the giant bird was airborne, banking into the night toward the jungle.

The cargo hold rattled and groaned, every rivet humming with vibration. Crates lined the walls in neat rows, shadows dancing across their stenciled surfaces. The air smelled of fuel and iron.

Weiss sat on a crate across from Honiael, his elbows on his knees, studying her like a predator sizing up prey. The blindfold hid her defiant glare, but he could feel it. With a grunt, he reached out and ripped the gag from her mouth.

Instantly, she erupted, a torrent of sharp-edged syllables in her native tongue— melodic and venomous all at once. Her voice filled the metal chamber with fire.

Weiss leaned back, letting her rage burn itself out with an impressed chuckle. When her voice cracked, he smiled coldly.

"I just want to talk," he said.

She hissed a curse, words like a poisoned flower.

He tilted his head, voice calm, coaxing. "Tell me about your world. Why is it your kind can slip into ours, but we've never been able to walk into yours?"

She stayed silent, breathing hard through her nose. Her lips curled. "You are not worthy!"

Weiss smiles in agreement. "You don't like the way I treat you? That's fine. It's simple. Cooperate." His tone softened, almost reasonable. "It doesn't have to be this hard."

Weiss stood, circling her slowly, his boots ringing against the metal deck.

His hand brushed her bare shoulder, cool skin beneath his fingers.

"You're… remarkable," he murmured, his eyes tracing the lines of her body. "What if we were to meet an arrangement? Humans. Elves. Working together." His voice gained heat and conviction.

"Think of it. A better world, built by both our races. No secrets. No walls."

He leaned close, his breath hot against her ear. "I want you to be comfortable. Don't you want to be comfortable?"

For a moment, she froze. Her breath hitched, body tense. Then, with a sudden shiver, she arched into him, her movements slow, deliberate, her lips parting as if to whisper consent.

Weiss smiled, lips brushing her neck with a

hint of desire—

In an instant, her head snapped back like a whip.

Bone met cartilage with a sharp *crack*. Pain exploded across his face. Weiss staggered back, clutching his nose as blood poured down over his lips.

Honiael roared an ancient chant, words dripping with fury, the chains rattling as she strained against them. Her voice rang with power, defiance echoing off every surface of the cargo bay.

Weiss's smile curdled into a snarl. He yanked his plasma pistol free, leveled it at her head, and pulled the trigger. The static bolt struck the back of her skull with a sizzling crack. Her body sagged, unconscious, still chained to the pallet.

Breathing hard, blood streaking his face, Weiss loomed over her limp form. With deliberate malice, he shoved the gag back between her lips and yanked the straps tight until the leather bit into her skin.

He wiped his nose on his sleeve, spat blood on the floor, and stormed toward the cockpit without another word.

Behind him, Honiael lay silent, the echo of her chant still ringing in the steel bones of the plane.

Chapter 33
The Path of the Olmec

The ship's soft hum was the only sound when Jack stirred awake. He blinked groggily, realizing Gemma was curled against him, her arms draped over his chest like she never meant to let go. For a long moment he just lay there, listening to the quiet rise and fall of her breath, the fragile peace they had carved out of chaos.

By the time they made their way to the control room, the faint aroma of synthesized food drifted in the air. Chris was already there, hunched over his tray, dark circles under his eyes. His laptop sat beside him, still tethered to the Aegis systems by a few lazy coils of cable.

Broken2 waited at the far end of the chamber, her humanoid form shimmering faintly in the glow of holographic screens. Gemma pressed close to Jack as they ate, the silent intimacy of touch stronger than any words. Chris, though, looked restless, his fork stabbing absentmindedly at the constructed food. Finally, he broke the silence.

"I dug into the databases last night," Chris said, his voice thin but sharp. "I found something about the Key. Coordinates. References. Old records. It points to… South America." He glanced at Broken2. "Something about a Meso-american empire."

Broken2 inclined her head. "The Olmec," she said, her voice low and resonant. "One of the great civilizations to rise on your world after the Aegis heart terraformed it. The first great civilizations were gifted with fragments of our knowledge and technology. For a time, they thrived, crafting cities, temples, and monuments that still whisper their presence today. Until the "others" arrived and genetically modified your original ancestors... but that is a story for another time."

She gestured, and a hologram shimmered into being—a colossal stone head, eyes weathered, lips curved in enigmatic silence.

"They were the last people known to have possession of the Key. But they feared it. Coveted it. Eventually they used it's technology to subjugate and enslave others. Wars erupted.

And when their empire crumbled, the Key was lost with them, buried in jungles where time devours all things."

Chris leaned forward, rubbing his temples. "So that's where we start looking."

Jack squeezed Gemma's hand. "If it's the only lead, then that's where we go."

Broken2's gaze lingered on each of them, as though memorizing their faces. Then she turned, beckoning them to follow. The hallway ahead rippled, shifting and stretching like a living maze. Walls folded away. A new doorway formed.

When it opened, they stepped into a cavernous hangar, their breath catching at the sight.

Sleek and black, its surface shimmering with blue veins of energy. Its shape was that of a boomerang sharpened into elegance, wings curved and lean, its form humming with restrained power.

"This is the Riftrunner," Broken2 said. Her voice was proud, but tinged with something else—something heavy. "She will carry you safely to Earth. She is fast, silent, and built for infiltration. But understand this—" Her form flickered slightly as she looked at them. "I cannot go with you. If you fall, the Aegis will need me to try again. You are not the first to seek the Key. You may not be the last."

Gemma looked at Jack, fear stirring in her

eyes. Chris's fists clenched at his sides, jaw tight.

Jack's hand curled around Gemma's. "We'll make it," Jack said, steady as stone. "We have to."

Broken2 only watched them, her expression unreadable, as the Riftrunner pulsed to life.

Chapter 34
The Bait

The cargo ramp of the C-5 groaned as the vehicles rolled into the sticky jungle air. Weiss stood at the edge, his hands shoved into his coat pockets, a fresh bandage strung crooked across his broken nose. Two swollen black eyes made his face look like a grotesque mask, but the smirk never left his lips.

He flicked a switch in his hand, holding it up so Honiael could see. The faint red light of the new collar around her neck blinked in time with Weiss's remote.

"Fashionable, don't you think?" Weiss said, voice gravelly from the swelling. "A little something to remind you of our... arrangement." He thumbed the switch, and the collar chirped with a warning beep. "One twitch of my finger, and... pop."

Honiael's eyes glowed faintly violet beneath her blindfold, her melodic voice muffled behind the gag. Weiss chuckled and waved a hand. "Let her off the pallet. I want her to stretch her legs before the fun starts."

The soldiers obeyed, yanking the straps free.

They kept her cuffed, dragging her limp but defiant body into the waiting Humvee. She was shoved onto her back as two men climbed in and pinned her with their weight. A third soldier gripped the wheel while Weiss claimed the passenger seat, leaning back smugly.

Ahead of them, an M1A1 Abrams tank rumbled to life, its turret swaying like a blunt predator's head. The tank's treads churned the earth, flattening trees and chewing through the jungle until a crude road formed.

The convoy moved forward, humid leaves whipping against armored steel, the stink of diesel choking out the natural scents of moss and rain.

Hours seemed to stretch into a fever dream of mechanical thunder and choking green.

Finally, the tank braked hard before an immense mound of earth and stone, half-swallowed by centuries of jungle. Vines draped its sides like the hair of a corpse, and at its base yawned a cavernous mouth, dark and beckoning.

"Home sweet home," Weiss muttered, stepping down from the Humvee. He lit a cigarette, shielding the flame with a trembling hand.

Around him, soldiers moved with mechanical efficiency—setting up a perimeter, clearing brush, stringing lights and heavy cables like they'd done it a hundred times before.

Honiael was dragged out of the Humvee and thrown to the mossy ground at Weiss's boots. Her restraints clicked loose, and the soldiers stepped back warily. She flexed her arms, standing with as much dignity as she could muster, the explosive collar gleaming at her throat.

Weiss crouched before her, the cigarette glowing between his fingers. His broken face twisted into something close to a grin. "Here's how it goes, sweetheart. You're going to walk into that cave, nice and slow, and you're going to show us where to step. Every trap, every beast, every little surprise the ancestors left behind—you're going to deal with it for us. And if you don't?" He tapped the switch against his palm, hard enough to make it beep again. "Well… we both know how that ends."

"A weapon?" Honiel pleads.

Weiss smiles and takes a machete from a soldier and cuts down a small tree, then lops it down into a stick before throwing it at her feet. "Do try to make it work. princess. Uncle Sam doesn't have resources to waste." She looks up at him with a hateful sneer and reluctantly picks up the stick.

The soldiers shifted uneasily, their rifles catching the dim light. The jungle around them buzzed with the calls of unseen creatures.

Weiss stood, flicking ash at her feet. "Lead the way, elf. Welcome to your new career —point woman for Uncle Sam."

He waved to the waiting squad, and their boots crunched into formation. Together, under the gaze of the overgrown mound, they turned toward the cavern that swallowed light itself.

And Weiss made sure Honiael stepped first.

Chapter 35
Into the Green

The cave swallowed them like the gullet of some ancient beast. Their boots echoed in the gloom, the heavy breath of the soldiers competing with the hum of fluorescent lanterns clipped to their vests.

The air smelled of stone, damp earth, and something older—like dust that hadn't been disturbed in a thousand years.

Honiael's collar beeped faintly with every step, the red light winking in the dark. She moved stiffly between two armed men, her gaze hard and unblinking.

As they descended deeper, the rough cavern walls shifted—rock giving way to geometry. Massive bricks jutted from the earth as though the jungle itself had tried to bury them.

Crumbling ruins, etched with indecipherable glyphs, protruded like bones from the walls.

Then the tunnel opened into a vast chamber. A great stone doorway loomed ahead, its arch supported by carved pillars, glyphs flickering with phosphorescent lichen.

Before it stood ten figures—native

tribesmen, their bodies painted in streaks of ochre and ash. At their center, an elder with hair white as ash leaned on a carved staff, his eyes glowing with the fire of authority.

The soldiers froze, hands tight on their rifles. Weiss smirked and stepped forward, hands open as if in peace. He inclined his head mockingly, then spoke in the tribes' language, his voice fluid, practiced.

The elder Shaman raised his staff, answering in a low, sonorous chant that rolled through the chamber like thunder. Though the words were foreign, their meaning was clear: **leave, or perish.**

Weiss glanced back at his men, grinning as if he'd just been told the punchline of a joke. "Apparently," he said dryly, "we're trespassing. And we must go."

He pivoted smoothly, walking back toward the squad, lighting another cigarette as if nothing were out of place. Then his voice turned hard, cold as stone.

"Well, you know your orders, men. No witnesses."

The soldiers moved in perfect unison. Rifles raised. The cavern filled with thunder. Honiael gasped, horrified, as bullets tore through unarmed flesh.

The tribesmen staggered and fell, painted bodies collapsing into the dust.

The Shaman alone stood upright, chest riddled with holes, blood soaking into the earth. Still, he tried to breathe, tried to curse them with his last strength.

Weiss exhaled a stream of smoke, looming over him. He pressed the muzzle of his plasma pistol to the man's forehead and smiled almost tenderly.

"Wrong answer."

The pistol barked a bolt of solid light and the Shaman's smoking head snapped back as his body crumpled to the ground.

Above the clouds, the Riftrunner howled through the atmosphere, fire streaking along its sleek black frame. Inside, the kids screamed with exhilaration as the ship tore into the sky and then leveled into a smooth glide.

Jack whooped, holding Gemma's hand tight. Chris clung to his seat, grinning despite his exhaustion.

Broken2 shimmered into being as a hologram at the front of the cockpit, her form glowing faintly blue. Her tone was calm, but heavy with warning.

"The Aegis has scanned your destination. Weiss is already there—with several units entrenched at the cave entrance. If you proceed, there may be lethal resistance."

The excitement in the cabin drained into a sober silence. Jack's jaw clenched. Gemma glanced at him nervously, then straightened with resolve. Chris nodded once, determination flaring in his tired eyes.

Jack spoke for them all. "Then we don't go in loud. We land nearby, sneak in, and get the key before Weiss even knows we're there."

Broken2 inclined her head, eyes bright with pride. "The Riftrunner will cloak as you approach. You will be shadows in the trees."

The ship shimmered out of sight as it descended into the jungle. Branches cracked beneath them as the sleek craft settled into a clearing, invisible as mist.

The hatch hissed open, humid air rushing in. Jack, Gemma, and Chris looked at each other-young faces, hard with new purpose. It was time.

Chapter 36
Into the Dark

The Riftrunner sat hidden in its clearing, jungle birds screaming overhead, mist curling through the branches. Inside, the air was heavy with anticipation.

Jack adjusted the gauntlet on his wrist and looked at Chris. "Chris, you're staying here. If Gem and I run into trouble, we'll need backup. Or a quick retreat."

Chris frowned. "Jack, I should be out there with you—"

"No," Jack cut him off. "We need someone watching our backs. That means you. If this goes bad, you're the only chance we've got."

Chris swallowed hard. His hands flexed against the console. Finally, he nodded. "... Fine. But don't think I'll just sit here twiddling my thumbs."

Jack stepped forward and pulled him into a hug.

Gemma did the same, wrapping her arms around Chris with a squeeze that lingered a heartbeat longer than usual. "We'll come back," she whispered.

Chris nodded stiffly, holding onto their warmth as long as he could.

Then Jack forced a grin. "Keep the engine warm for us."

"Christopher, use the interface visor and launch the Riftrunner's Orb. I will show you how to use it." Broken2 chirps over the comm.

Jack and Gem stepped toward the hatch, as Chris slid the sleek visor over his eyes. At once, his senses bled away from his body and into a black metallic sphere hovering above the jungle canopy. Every rustle, every shimmer of light bent differently from this perspective. He was the orb now—silent, invisible, everywhere at once.

The hatch hissed open, spilling humid air into the cabin. Jack and Gemma stumbled into the green.

Their armor shimmered, surfaces rippling as the nanites adjusted to mimic leaves, bark, shadows. Within moments they melted into the jungle. Chris's orb drifted after them like a ghost.

The heat was suffocating, the insects relentless. Jack pushed forward, his improvised nano blade sang through the thick vines, parting with the sweep of his gauntlet's edge. Gemma stayed close, listening to the exotic animals that surrounded them.

After a long silence, she said softly, "Jack…there's something I need to tell you. About a dream I had."

"Now?" Jack muttered, brushing aside a curtain of ferns.

"Yes, now." Her voice wavered. "It wasn't just a dream. It felt real. I saw us… together, safe. And then—" she hesitated, "—something dark. Something huge. It killed you, Jack. I watched you die."

Jack chuckled without slowing his pace. "Gem, it was just stress. We've all been through hell. Your brain's just…processing it."

"Processing?" she snapped, grabbing his arm and spinning him around. "You think I don't know the difference between a nightmare and a vision? Don't just brush me off, Jack!"

Her eyes flashed with anger and fear. Jack opened his mouth to respond—

—and the indifferent ground gave way.

The loose jungle floor crumbled beneath their boots. Jack and Gemma screamed as they plummeted into a shaft of darkness, arms flailing, the canopy above shrinking into a jagged circle of light.

Above, the recon orb hovered. Chris,

immersed in its vision, froze.

"Where are you—?!" His voice cracked as he spun the orb frantically, scanning the empty jungle. Then he saw it—the raw, fresh wound in the earth.

And then the comms came alive. Screams.

Jack and Gemma's voices echoing up from the darkness, sharp and terrified. The sound of metal striking stone. A screech—inhuman, high-pitched, hungry.

"Jack! Gemma!" Chris shouted, heart hammering. His hands shook as he fought to steady the orb. "Talk to me! What's happening down there?!"

Static answered him, broken by another scream.

Without hesitation, Chris hurled the orb into the chasm, plunging into the dark after them.

Chapter 37
Ghosts in the Ruins

The orb skimmed through the crevasse, ricocheting off jagged stone as Chris fought to steady it. Each impact jolted his vision, the visor rattling against his head.

Below, Jack and Gemma tumbled through the abyss in a blur of armor and sparks, their bodies slamming against the walls as the endless drop consumed them.

"Jack!" Gemma's scream tore through the comms, raw and panicked. "We're going to die!"

"Not—if—I—can—help it!" Jack's voice broke with each brutal bounce, but he forced himself to sound steady. "We'll—live—just—hold on!"

"Hold on to what?!" Gem shrieked.

"Anything!" Jack barked, his attempt at humor cracking under the weight of fear. He smashed hard against the wall, armor sparking.

Chris's orb dove after them, skimming past protruding stone and shattered ledges, its sensors struggling to keep pace. His heart pounded in his ears as their voices filled the comms, each impact louder than the last.

Then the crevasse opened into a vast, impossible space.

A ruined city sprawled in the darkness, towers crumbled and streets split wide with age. Moss and fungus glowed faintly on weathered stone, painting the abyss in sickly green light.

The ground surged upward.

"Brace!" Jack shouted.

They hit hard.

Their armored bodies slammed into the ancient street like artillery strikes. Rock exploded outward, carving fresh craters into the ruins. Dust and gravel billowed up in choking clouds.

Chris dove the orb down, sensors whirling. "Jack! Gemma! Answer me—please—come on, don't do this to me!"

For a moment, nothing.

Then Gemma stirred. A low groan crackled through the comms as her armored frame pushed upright. "Ow. Ow. Ow..." She paused. "...Okay, that was awful."

Broken2 chirps into the comms "Inertial dampener shields absorbed 99.98% of your impact. Technically, you can withstand a terminal velocity impact of a planet with a gal rating of 3,400 from orbit at terminal velocity."

Jack's voice followed, strained but alive. "What the hell does that mean B2? Ugh...At least we're still breathing. Still in one piece." He rolled to his knees and stood, shaking dust from his armor plates. "Guess that worked out."

Chris replies "What Broken2 means is, that we can dive from orbit with our armor and hit the ground without dying."

Gemma leaned into Jack, her voice trembling between tears and nervous laughter. "I thought we were dead."

Jack wrapped an arm around her shoulders, pulling her in close. "Not today." Chris exhaled a shaky laugh through the comms, relief flooding his tone. "You two are unbelievable."

But then his voice sharpened. "Uh—guys? I hate to ruin the moment, but... we're not alone."

The orb's light swept across the street.

A figure stood there, pale and still, as if he had always been part of the ruins. A pale shaman draped in tattered cloth, leaning on a staff, his face unreadable in the gloom.

He raised a long finger to his lips—silent, commanding. Then he turned, pointing toward the looming silhouette of a step pyramid in the distance. Its broken stairways vanished into shadow, the yawning mouth of a cave gaping at its base.

Jack and Gemma exchanged uneasy glances.

When they looked back, the old man was gone.

Chris's voice came fast and uncertain. "I—I don't understand. He didn't even register on sensors. No heat. No readings. Nothing. You guys saw him, Right?"

A chill sank into the silence between them. Gemma shivered inside her suit. Jack steadied his grip on her arm. Without another word, they turned toward the pyramid and began moving, the orb gliding close at their heels.

The ruins swallowed their footsteps as they entered the dark.

Chapter 38
The Labyrinth

The air inside the labyrinth was thick, stale, and stinking of death. Weiss led the way with Honiael in front, her explosive collar glowing faint red in the gloom, its beeping reminder of her leash with every step. The soldiers kept their rifles raised, boots crunching across dust that hadn't been disturbed in centuries.

Honiael walked gracefully, her ancient violet eyes darting across the walls, the floor, the ceiling. She noticed the faint trip-lines hidden in the dark. She sidestepped one pressure plate, letting her bare toes land silently on safer stone. She smiles to herself.

Weiss trailed close, too focused on the massive glyphs carved into the walls. Twisting figures writhed in his flashlight—women bound to altars, throats slit by obsidian knives, rivers of blood painted in geometric precision.

All centered around a golden diamond. His lip curled, half in fascination, half in disgust. "Perhaps?" He mutters with a sneer his lucky steps avoiding the ancient trigger.

Then inevitable intervened.

One of the soldiers just behind him, unknowingly stepped onto the square slab. *Click.* They collectively froze.

The floor trembled, and in a flash of ancient machinery springing to life, giant obsidian blades scythed through the corridor. Three men were shredded by scythian blades in an instant—torsos severed, blood spraying the glyphs as though the murals themselves demanded new offerings. The survivors froze in horror, aiming their gun lights at the ribbons of flesh at their feet.

The final blade whipped past Weiss so close it tore his sleeve. He flinched, clutching the remote to Honiael's collar, his breath sharp and ragged.

Honiael only smiled, her voice calm and sharp as a dagger.

"Oops. I must have missed one."

Weiss snarled, shoving the remote inches from her face.

"You miss another, elf, and I'll wipe your smirk off myself."

They pressed deeper. The soldiers, fewer now, moved like ghosts, eyes wide, rifle lights casting long shadows in front of them. Honiael slowed, studying the ground.

Then—deliberately—she slammed her heel into the rotting wooden floor.

The corridor gave way beneath them. With a groan of ancient rotting beams, the floor shattered and they all tumbled, weapons clattering into darkness.

They unceremoniously land in a black glass tunnel with a crunch. Weiss screamed in anger as he lost hold of the detonator, the black switch bouncing and skittering away. The soldiers scrambled after it, but gravity took them first.

The smooth obsidian chute swallowed them whole.

They slid downward, quickly accelerating at breakneck speeds, sparks flashing as their gear scraped against the glass like surface. Honiael bent her knees and rode the slope on her feet, the stick in her hand skidding behind her like her rudder. Her stance is balanced and fluid like a falcon on a perch.

Weiss clawed uselessly, tumbling end over end, his hand reaching for the detonator as it spun and bounced from his fingertips.

She grabbed for the remote—he grabbed back. The two struggled, snarling, elbowing, their fight echoing in the tunnel as the chute screamed by.

Then the obsidian channel ahead split open, revealing a final paper-thin, obsidian blade slicing across the chute like a guillotine.

"We're dead...AAAAAAAH!" one soldier shouted—just before the trap cleaved him in an instant, bisecting him in a single clean stroke, a crimson pool splashes down the slick slope as his halved remains flop helplessly down the chute with the other two spinning soldiers.

Weiss and Honiael rolled together, narrowly avoiding another glassy blade, and sail into the open darkness as they fire out of the chute and into a vast darkness below.

Seconds later, Their bodies slammed into black stone with sickening thuds, groans echoing.

Silence followed—ominous, crushing.

Then the collar beeped again in the dark.

Chapter 39
The Roar in the Dark

The obsidian hall stretched like a vein into the depths of the ruined city, its smooth walls broken only by countless open chutes spiraling down into darkness. Every footstep echoed as if the very stone were listening.

Chris's orb glided low over the floor, its sensors humming. In his visor, a pulse of sound flared on the scan—low, steady, like a thunderous heartbeat wrapped in static. "Hey… I've got something," Chris muttered. "It's rhythmic, electrified… but I don't know what it means."

Before Jack could answer, Broken2's calm voice slid into their comms.

"That, Christopher, is a nano-signature. The roar of communication between nanite colonies. This one is primordial… crafted by men. Crafted by the key. Caution is advised."

Chris's brow furrowed behind his visor. "How is that even possible?"

Gemma's voice broke in, sharp and tight with unease.

"And exactly what should we be cautious of, B2?!"

The answer came not from Broken2, but from the shadows.

Something blacker than the obsidian itself erupted from a chute—a blur of jagged edges and writhing limbs. It slammed into Jack, knocking him off his feet and dragging him screaming into the dark.

"JACK!" Gemma shrieked, her voice splitting over the comms. Chris spun the orb wildly, scanning the walls, every chute alive with echoes of movement. Sparks burst from one tunnel, then another— flashes of violent light, the sound of metal on metal.

Then—BOOM.

Jack crashed back through the wall, obsidian shards scattering across the floor. He staggered upright, armor sparking, chest heaving.

"I think I found it the signal..." he rasped jokingly, trying to steady his friends.

But behind Gemma, the darkness rippled. The nano-beast slithered out, its form half-liquid, half-armor, its claws gleaming like serrated obsidian. Its eyeless head tilted, and it lunged.

"RUN!" Jack roared.

Gemma spun just in time, the claws slicing air where her head had been. Jack seized

her hand and pulled, their boots pounding
as the armor surged power into their legs.
They sprinted, knees like pistons, tearing
down the hall with inhuman speed.

Chris's orb zipped after them, its lenses
catching glimpses of the creature in
pursuit. The beast slammed against the
walls, its bladed body tearing great chunks
of obsidian free, showering shards down
on them as it screeched.

"How do we kill it?!" Jack shouted over the
comms.

Broken2's voice came sharp and clinical.
"You must destroy its nano-core. It will be
an artifact much like mine. Always hidden
in the densest part of its body.
Concentrated attacks are essential."

Jack ducked as another claw sliced across
the hall, sparks showering.

"We can't do it here—there isn't enough
room!" he yelled back.

Gemma's voice cracked with panic.
"What do we do, Jack?!"

"Keep running!" Chris shouted, his orb
skimming beside them as the beast's roar
filled the tunnel as his thrashing maw
snaps at them in desperation.

Chapter 40
Blood and Shadows

Honiael rolled out of the chute like a cat, landing light on her feet. Behind her, Weiss and the last of his soldiers slammed down in a heap, bone and armor crunching against the obsidian street. Bits of red rain pattered after them—blood from those who hadn't survived the descent.

Weiss groaned, dragging himself upright, his once-perfect uniform shredded and his face still swollen and bruised. Honiael advanced without hesitation, her stick gripped tight in her hand. She stalked toward him like an executioner.

Weiss, still half-propped against the stone, raised the remote, thumb resting casually on the trigger. His smile twisted beneath his bandaged nose.

"Not so fast, princess. We're so close. It'd be a shame for you to lose your head before you get to see the key."

Honiael froze, fury in her violet eyes.

Behind them, one of the surviving soldiers scrambled to help his comrade sit up—only to see the man's leg gone below the knee. The wounded soldier screamed until the other coolly raised his rifle and put a round in his skull. The echo cracked through the ruins.

"Splendid," Weiss sneered. "More glory for us."

The soldier gave a grim nod—then froze, his flashlight beam rising.

Weiss followed the light and his jaw fell open.

A black titan loomed in the chamber, an obsidian king carved from nightmare. Its upturned hand held a single object: a golden chevron, humming softly, hovering just above the stone.

Weiss shoved Honiael aside like refuse and staggered forward, transfixed. "It's here... it's really here." He waved his plasma pistol. "Collect it!" he barked at his soldier.

The man slung his rifle, climbing the statue's leg with practiced ease, one hand reaching for the prize.

Weiss lit a cigarette, eyes never leaving the chevron. His swollen grin widened. "Almost mine."

Then the sound came.

A scream—not human, not earthly. The shriek of metal tearing and glass breaking, followed by frantic voices in English, panicked and raw.

"JACK!"

"GEMMA, MOVE!"

Jack and Gemma burst from a side corridor, smashing into a glass-paneled wall and skidding across the chamber floor in their armor. Chris's orb zipped after them, bobbing into the expanse above like a frantic firefly.

The black nano-beast exploded through the tunnel after them seconds later, its body writhing blades and gnashing limbs. It roared, the sound a metallic avalanche, and the chamber shook with resonance.

Honiael seized her chance—she lashed out with a precise kick, knocking Weiss's detonator from his hand, flinging it off into the shadows.

Then jumping away and fading into the dark.

Weiss panicked, jerking his plasma pistol up as both he and the remaining soldier opened fire on Jack, Gemma, and the beast alike.

The skilled soldier perched on the statue's knees kept his aim tight, slamming round after round into the beast. Shards of nano-matter burst off with each hit. The monster turned, snarled, and launched itself up the statue like liquid shadow.

The soldier barely screamed before it shredded him apart, chunks of armor and flesh raining down. The creature devoured what was left, its maw tearing with wet crunches. A rain of blood spattered the chamber—splattering Weiss's uniform, dripping from his hair.

Weiss, trembling but laughing wildly, pulled a sleek injector from his belt and jammed it into his thigh. His pupils dilated, veins crawling up his face like black lightning.

"You're not the only ones with alien tech, shitheads!" he screamed, froth at his lips, as the golden chevron hovered quietly above them like royalty watching a duel for its favor.

Chapter 41
Demon in Red

High above the shattered chamber, Chris guided the orb in frantic arcs, his hands sweating under the visor. The chaos below looked like a nightmare come alive. Jack and Gemma scrambled across broken obsidian, the golden chevron pulsed brighter, and the nano-beast writhed around the colossal statue like a dragon claiming its hoard.

"B2—what can I do to help?!" Chris shouted, his voice breaking. "Does this thing have weapons?!"

Broken2's calm voice filled the comms. "Yes, Christopher. My orbs can project interference fields. A concentrated resonant signal beam can dissolve nanite bonds… but you must get close."

Chris swallowed hard, clutching the controls. "Close. Right. No pressure." Below, the beast shrieked as its body flexed around the statue's obsidian form. Jack dragged Gemma behind a fallen slab.

"Where's Weiss?!" Jack yelled, his voice echoing.

Before Gemma could answer, the shadows answered for them.

A monstrous red arm erupted from the dark, claws clamping around the beast's throat. The nano-creature convulsed as it was wrenched free from the statue and hurled into the street, crashing in a storm of shards.

Weiss stepped into the light—or rather, something wearing Weiss. His body was engulfed in molten red nanite armor, jagged and horned, wings unfurling like a demon ripped from hell. His swollen, battered human face was gone, replaced by a screaming crimson helm.

"YOU THOUGHT YOU COULD BEAT MEEEE!" his voice thundered, not human anymore but a distorted roar of gurgling metal.

The nano encased Weiss raised his massive fist and brought it down again and again on the pinned beast. Each strike exploded shards of black glass and sprays of writhing nanites. The street trembled beneath the impacts.

Jack and Gemma froze, breath caught in their throats.

"What the hell is that?" Gem whispered.

"That's uh... Mecha-Weiss?," Jack said, voice low. "Or what's left of him."

"Jack, what do we do?"

Chris's voice cut in over comms, desperate but steady. "Hit where he hits! The core's there—he's showing you the weak spot!"

The orb dove, streaking down like a black comet. Its lenses glowed and unleashed lances of blue-white energy at the flailing beast. The beams sizzled, eating holes through its body. The creature shrieked and twisted, striking out with barbed limbs.

Weiss snarled, swatting at the orb with a massive clawed hand.

The impact sent Chris spinning, his vision blurring in the visor as the orb spiraled into the air. Jack and Gemma screamed his name.

"Chris! Stay with us!"

"I'm fine!" he lied, steadying the orb with trembling hands. He jerked the beam back on target as Jack and Gemma burst from cover, plasma bolts erupting from their gauntlets.

Together they poured fire into the clash of monsters, their shots carving through shadow and crimson alike.

For one fleeting moment, it seemed they might actually tip the battle.

Then Weiss laughed. A deep, monstrous laugh that rattled the walls. He plunged both hands into the beast's chest, nanite claws sinking deep. With a savage wrench, he tore out a pulsing black core—spherical, writhing, alive.

The beast screamed one last time as Weiss crushed the core in his fist. Its body convulsed, then dissolved into nothing, fragments scattering like ash in the wind.

Jack and Gemma stood frozen, horror-struck.

The red giant turned toward them. And charged.

"MOVE!" Jack shoved Gemma aside just as Weiss's massive form thundered forward.

Chris's orb launched from the shadows, its beam cutting through the chamber and burning holes straight through Weiss's chest and helm.

The crimson shell melted away, and for an instant Weiss's battered human face was revealed inside—eyes wild with fury, twisted into something almost unrecognizable.

Weiss roared, snatched the orb midair, and slammed it into the obsidian wall. The orb detonated in a plasma explosion that rocked the chamber. Jack and Gemma were hurled across the street, smashing into a jagged wall.

Far away, aboard the Riftrunner, Chris slumped unconscious in his seat. The visor flickered with static as blood trickled from his nose and mouth and onto the console. In the ruined city below, the laughter of the red demon filled the darkness.

Chapter 42
The Elf and the Demon

From her perch high on a shattered spire, Honiael crouched low, the crude stick clutched in her hands. The golden chevron shimmered in its obsidian cradle below, glowing like a star caught in stone. She narrowed her eyes, watching the battle rage across the ruins.

Now is my chance, she thought, her heart hammering.

Below, Jack and Gemma fought like cornered wolves. Weiss—encased in his shrieking crimson shell—moved like a titan through the broken city.   His strikes cratered walls, his claws shredded glass streets into rivers of shards. Jack and Gemma darted through the storm, their armor glowing as they fired volley after volley of plasma fire, forcing him back step by step.

Jack rolled across the rubble and raised both hands, his gauntlets spitting a line of burning plasma that splashed against Weiss's armored chest. Weiss staggered, but only for a moment.

Gemma dove in, scooping up a fallen chunk of black nanite debris, her suit reshaping it into a crackling blade. She spun, slashing across Weiss's leg, sparks and nanite blood spraying as the monster roared in pain.

"Now, Gem!" Jack shouted.

Together they unleashed a crossfire, bolts hammering into the same spot in Weiss's chest.

The armor sizzled, molten cracks spreading across it like glowing veins. Weiss screamed, voice warping into a hellish bellow.

Then he moved faster than their eyes could follow.

He backhanded Jack across the plaza, sending him crashing through a jagged wall. Before Gemma could fire again, Weiss's massive hand clamped around her torso. He slammed her down, pinning her under his clawed foot.

The obsidian street spider-webbed beneath her armor as she cried out, her suit sparking under the pressure.

Jack scrambled to his feet, plasma cannon sparking in his palm, but Weiss's other hand clamped around his head, lifting him effortlessly. Jack's vision blurred as his skull was slowly crushing like an eggshell in a vice.

Gemma whimpered and squealed, her helmet groaning as cracks spread across the visor. "Jack—!"

"Hold on, Gemma!" Jack yelled, straining against the crushing grip. "Everything is going to work out! Stay with me, Gem!"

She sobbed, her breath ragged. "Jack…"

Weiss laughed—a deep, maniacal roar that rattled the ruined city. "NOW YOU WILL SEE TRUE POWER!!" His claws dug deeper, armor screeching as he crushed them both.

Jack screamed in defiance. Gemma screamed in pain.

Then a shadow fell from above.

Honiael.

The elf girl landed like a thunderclap on Weiss's shoulders, both hands gripping the crude stick.   With a cry that shook the ruins, she drove its jagged tip down with all her weight. The wooden shaft punched through his exposed throat, tearing into flesh and nanite alike. With a heave she drove it deep into his torso and ripped it out savagely. Black protoblood geysered into the air, spraying across her and Weiss as he roared in frustrated agony.

He reached up with one massive claw, tearing her from his shoulders like a doll.

With a brutal swing, he hurled her to the ground. She struck hard, her body crumpling and still.

Weiss turned back to finish Jack—only to find his prey slipping through his grasp like smoke.

Broken2's voice thundered through their comms:

"Phase shifters engaged."

Jack's body melted through Weiss's crushing hand, his form flickering into intangibility.

At the same instant, Weiss's foot passed straight through Gemma, his stomp shattering the street as she rolled free. She gasped in shock, armor sparking but intact.

Jack yanked her to her feet, dragging her away as Weiss stumbled, clutching at the spurting wound in his throat. Black ichor sprayed in violent bursts.

"Stay here!" Jack barked, pushing Gemma back against the wall.

Jack sprinted toward Honiael's small, broken form. Weiss roared and lurched forward toward Honiael's motionless body out of pure revenge, blood trailing behind him in great spurting arcs. But his steps faltered. His towering red shell sparked, splitting apart.

With one final step, Weiss collapsed face-first into a jagged ledge, crushing his skull with a loud crunch. Jack deftly sprints and slides, scooping Honiael gently into his arms carrying her from underneath the faltering behemoth Weiss.

Her delicate body was streaked with violet and black blood, a purple trickle running from her temple. She didn't stir.

The obsidian cracked, and Weiss's body slid limply into the street below leaving a smear of what was once his head on the shelf above. His crimson armor sizzled, burning away to ash, leaving behind nothing but a blackened skeleton steaming in the dust.

Silence fell, broken only by the distant drip of water and the hum of the golden chevron high above.

"Jack!" Gemma called, running to his side, her voice trembling.

Jack stood, cradling the strange, unconscious girl. His arms shook from the weight of battle, but he held her steady.

Gemma's eyes widened as she saw the pointed ears, and the alien beauty in her face even through blood and dirt. She gasped softly. "Who… who is she?"

Jack looked down at Honiael, then back to

Gemma. "I don't know."

Gemma reached out, brushing a strand of the girl's blood-matted hair from her cheek. Her voice was hushed, reverent. "What *is* she?"

Jack's gaze hardened. "I don't know. But she saved our lives." He shifted the girl gently into Gemma's arms. "And we are not leaving her here."

The three of them stood in the ruins—the last echo of Weiss's laugh still lingering in the shadows—while above them, the golden chevron shimmered like a silent watcher.

Chapter 43
Surrounded

The chamber echoed with silence after Weiss's fall, the blackened skeleton still smoldering in the rubble. Jack and Gemma stood frozen for a heartbeat, their armor sparking in faint pulses of blue. Then Jack reached up, retracting his helmet. His sweat-slick face was lit by the glow of the golden chevron. Gemma mirrored him, her helmet peeling back with a soft hiss.

Without words, they grabbed each other, lips colliding in a desperate, bruising kiss. For one blissful moment the world and its horrors melted away.

Gemma broke first, her eyes wide. "Chris! What about Chris!?" She slapped her comms, her voice rising with panic. "Chris! Can you hear me? Where are you!?"

Only static answered.

Jack's chest tightened. He looked at Gemma, and she saw the worry in his eyes, though he forced it down. "We'll get to Chris. But first—we finish this. Let's get the key so we can get out of here."

Gemma nodded reluctantly.

Gemma carries Honiael slung over her back with nano tentacles wrapping her body gently.

Jack scaled the massive obsidian statue, its black surface slick with blood and dust. His armored fingers dug into cracks as he climbed.

At the top, the golden chevron floated above the titan's palm, humming with alien resonance. Carefully, reverently, Jack reached out and closed his hands around it. The air vibrated as he touched it, his armor lighting briefly before it dimmed again. The key was warm, alive, and pulsed faintly in his grip.

He slung it across his back , his armor grabbing onto it. "Let's move."

They climbed their way up to the chute, and began walking up the long slope with jagged armored toes gripping into the glass. The climb seemed endless, their breaths echoing inside their helmets as they carried the elf girl and the key toward the faint glow above.

At last, they emerged into the surface tunnels. A rank stench of blood filled their suits.

Gemma froze. Her voice cracked. "Jack... look. Is that...?"

The bodies of the native tribesmen lay scattered across the cavern floor. Strong men, all cut down where they stood. Jack crouched beside the familiar body of the old shaman. His eyes, still wide, stared blankly into nothing. A blackened hole centered through his head.

Jack pressed a gauntlet laden hand gently over the man's face, closing his eyelids. "...I think so. Looks like he's been dead for a while too."

Gemma's brow furrowed. "But… how? We saw him down there. He—he helped us."

Jack shook his head, rising to his feet. His voice was heavy. "I don't know, Gem." He glanced back down at the old man, solemnly whispering. "Thank you, old man."

They stepped out of the cave mouth, eyes squinting against the flood of jungle sunlight.

Then the light shifted.

Jack and Gemma froze as their visors adjusted. Before them stretched an army: Weiss's forces, arrayed in a semicircle, weapons raised. A dozen Humvees lined the clearing, 50 cal machine guns bearing down at them. At the center, the colossal barrel of an M1A1 Abrams tank pointed directly at Jack's head, humming with lethal readiness.

A hundred rifles locked on them with mechanical precision.

Gemma swallowed hard, her voice trembling. "Uuuh, Jack…"

Jack tightened his fists. His voice was grim. "Yeah. I see them."

The jungle fell silent but for the faint hiss of the tank's engine.

The hatch at the top of the Abrams banged open, and a Dark Wing commander rose from it. His face was hard as steel as he drew in a breath and raised his hand. "Ready…!" he barked, his voice carrying over the troops.

Jack shoved Gemma behind him, snapping a shimmering nano-shield into existence. He braced, knowing it wouldn't last against this kind of firepower.

Then the sky ripped open.

A thunderous blast of plasma shot down from above, melting a molten hole through the tank's turret. The machine bucked violently before its ammunition ignited. The explosion tore the tank apart, shredding the commander in an instant.

Jack and Gemma didn't hesitate—they opened fire, their plasma blasters ripping into the confused ranks. Soldiers scattered, screaming, as Humvees erupted in fire.

"LOOK! It's CHRIS!" Gemma shouted, pointing skyward.

The Riftrunner descended through the smoke, its sleek frame shimmering as plasma cannons roared. A dazzling array of energy bolts lit up the clearing, tearing through vehicles and scattering men like leaves in a storm.

Chris's voice crackled over the comms, raw and furious. "You're not touching them!" His scream carried with the fury of someone who had seen enough.

Jack and Gemma ducked low as the battlefield became a hurricane of fire. Men and steel alike were hurled into the air, vanishing in smoke and flame.

And then—silence.

The clearing was a ruin, filled with twisted vehicles and scorched earth. Not a single soldier stirred.

The Riftrunner landed in the smoldering debris field, its ramp hissing open. Jack and Gemma sprinted across the blackened ground, Honiael clutched between them. They scrambled aboard just as the ramp sealed.

The ship's engines flared. In an instant, the Riftrunner lifted from the wreckage and vanished, cloaked in invisibility.

Below, the old shaman stands stoically at the cave entrance, holding the palm of his hand toward them, chanting prayers of gratitude, as the Riftrunner evaporate from sight.

Chapter 44
The Key

The Riftrunner shimmered into dock, scorched and battered but alive. Inside, the three young warriors stumbled down the ramp, armor dented, visors cracked, weapons nearly spent. Jack cradled their prize—the golden Chevron Key—like it was made of glass.

Broken2 was waiting. Her tall frame stood still, luminous eyes glowing in the command bay's half-light. For once, her expression seemed almost… warm.

"You did it," she said. "Bring it here."

Jack hands the Key to Broken2 who laughs as she holds it. "The silly humans gilded it in gold. No wonder I couldn't detect it anymore." Broken2 raises a tendril toward the key as a laser burns the gold from it's surface, revealing it's black, mirrored skin.

She then gently placed the Key into the cradle at the heart of the console.

The effect was instant.

The Aegis shuddered—then roared as the key pedestal is slowly engulfed into the floor. Lights ignited across its endless halls. Energy cascaded through conduits like veins filled with fire. The deck vibrated underfoot as the ship seemed to awaken fully for the first time in an eon.

"Full power has been restored," Broken2 confirmed satisfactorily, her voice reverberating like a choir. "The Key will take several days to fully reintegrate with the Aegis Core, but its heart beats again."

Relief washed over the crew. Gemma leaned against Jack, closing her eyes. Chris exhaled shakily, still pale from the strain of piloting the Riftrunner.

"Broken2…" Gemma's voice cracked. "This girl. She's—"

Jack carefully laid the unconscious elf onto a slab. Her violet blood was still wet against his gauntlets. "She saved us. Don't let her die."

The med bay unfolded around them: walls shifting, machines rising, liquid-metal tendrils unfurling. Crystalline prongs hummed as they scanned Honiael's fragile frame. Chris steadied himself, sweat streaking his face. He moved to help, guided by Broken2's calm instructions.

Gemma hovered close. "What *is* she?" she whispered.

Broken2 paused, hands hovering above the glowing console. Her eyes dimmed and flared. "She is not a true alien like you imagine. Her body... contains particles... not from this universe. She is threaded with matter from an alternate dimension."

Jack's brows furrowed. "Then how is she here?"

"I cannot say." Broken2's voice lowered, almost reverent. "But the Aegis Core will analyze her further. For now, she is stable."

The machines hissed as violet blood ceased to flow, replaced by strands of faint light weaving into her veins. Honiael's breathing steadied, her chest rising and falling softly. Broken2 disarms the explosive collar from the strange woman's thin neck and absorbs it into her body.

Gemma brushed damp hair from the elf's face and whispered, "You're safe now." Hours later, the crew stood in the command chamber.

Above them, a vast hologram bloomed— the full glory of the Aegis Core revealed at last. Its shields crackled endlessly, celestial and terrifying, its ancient armor glowing with renewed power.

"In a few days," Broken2 said, "we will have the last known trajectory of the Aegis parent ship. Its trail may lead us to truths long buried."

Jack stepped forward, shoulders squared despite the pain still stitched into his bones. "And us? What happens to us?" Broken2's gaze turned upon them, patient and sharp. "Until then, you rest. And you train. You are no longer children, Gemma, Chris and your new friend should return home soon."

"Home?!" Chris yells. Gemma holds onto Jack and looks him in the eyes...

"Wherever you go, Jack Tengu, I'm going too."

"Well that settles it!" Jack smiles as their lips meet with loving gratitude.

Gemma slipped her hand into Jack's. Chris stood beside them, pale but proud. For a brief moment, silence carried weight —not despair, but something like destiny.

Far away.

At Dark Wing headquarters, the air smelled of cold steel and ozone.

The General sat behind his desk, iron hands folded.

His soldier entered, eyes grim, and set down a single object: a scorched black dog tag. The name etched on it: **WEISS**.

"No survivors, sir," the soldier said.

The General's lip curled. He leaned back, breath hissing through his teeth. "Failure is… unacceptable." He pressed a comm switch. "Summon the doctor."

Beneath the fortress, the doctor guided him into a cavernous chamber. The floor vibrated with the thrum of hidden engines. Massive glass vats lined the walls, each filled with pale fluid. Inside floated shapes —thousands—each identical.

The doctor slid the dog tag into a slot. A machine hissed, gears grinding. One vat bubbled violently as its liquid drained. The glass split apart.

From the mist stepped a man—tall, muscled, gray eyes smoldering with hate. Weiss.

The doctor's face split into a grin. "Glad to have you back, Captain Weiss!" The Doctor shakily hands him a cigarette and a lighter.

Weiss lifted his head slowly. Protoplasma trickles from his jaw. His lips peeled into a sneer, as he lights the cigarette.